P9-CEJ-020

OTHER TITLES IN THE SMART NOVELS SERIES:

SAT VOCABULARY
● ● ● ● ● ● ● ● ● ● ● ● ● ●

BUSTED

SUN-KISSED

VAMPIRE DREAMS

RAVE NEW WORLD

S.C.A.M.

U.S. HISTORY
● ● ● ● ● ● ● ● ● ● ●

VOLUME ONE: A TIME FOR WITCHES

VOLUME TWO: SHADES OF BLUE AND GRAY

VOLUME THREE: RECKLESS REVOLUTION

VOLUME FOUR: GILDED DELIRIUM

d

r

ls

BY RYAN NERZ

smart novels
SAT VOCABULARY

**SPARK
NOTES**

For Aunt Debbie, Amy Rose, and Claire Ciserella

by Ryan Nerz

© 2004, 2005, 2008 by Spark Publishing

All rights reserved. No part of this publication may be reproduced, stored in a retrieval system, or transmitted, in any form or by any means, electronic, mechanical, photocopying, recording, or otherwise, without prior written permission from the publisher.

SPARKNOTES is a registered trademark of SparkNotes LLC.

Spark Publishing
A Division of Barnes & Noble
120 Fifth Avenue
New York, NY 10011
www.sparknotes.com

ISBN-13: 978-1-4114-0082-5
ISBN-10: 1-4114-0082-8

Please submit changes or report errors to www.sparknotes.com/errors.

Printed and bound in the United States

20 19 18 17 16 15 14 13 12 11

SAT is a registered trademark of the College Entrance Examination Board, which was not involved in the production of, and does not endorse, this book.

ACT is a registered trademark of the ACT, Inc., which was not involved in the production of, and does not endorse, this book.

September 3: Uncle Sam's Birthday

So, the first day of school is a good time to start a new diary, right? At least, I thought so last night when I bought this book—back when I actually thought things would be different this year. I was convinced that after my recent leap up the high school **hierarchy** to Junior with Popular Boyfriend status, not to mention my summer-long fitness/tanning campaign, I would no longer be Invisible Girl. And somehow I guess I thought that me being different would make everything else different too.

Okay, so that was a little **naïve**. After one day back at Columbus High, I can say that nothing's changed much at all. The preps stick with the preps, the hoods with the hoods. Doe-eyed freshmen rove in packs, holding their books with both hands to avoid having them dumped. **Haughty** seniors pretend they're having more fun than the rest of us. In classes, teachers make us say our names out loud and something about ourselves. The snippets of hallway conversation overheard are as **banal** as ever—"Yo, I'm bagging fifth period," or "Did you see what Sara/Macy/Gina/whoever is actually *wearing* today?"

Only one thing's different—Luke Barton. The new kid. He's from California. I got press clippings about him all day. In homeroom, Jenny Cassell, a tireless socialite who has sat **adjacent** to me in homeroom since seventh grade, drew an audience with her description: "He's this totally hot skateboarding, movie-star type with a reddish-blond afro and Salvation Army style, with expensive sneakers and jeans that are perfectly worn in. And he's all **aloof**, like he's in on some secret you're not."

---

hierarchy: chain of command
naïve: inexperienced

haughty: proud
banal: bland

adjacent: next to
aloof: standoffish

By far the most **ebullient** description I heard was from my best friend. Nikki's first words to me sounded like something straight out of *Star Wars*: "Luke will be mine." She had already turned him into a savior. "See Fran, this is exactly what I was talking about! Remember when I said I needed a change? Well it's arrived. He's here. Luke Barton's the thing that's been missing for me in this town. He's going to be a **catalyst** for change in my life—I can already see it."

Nikki moved here from Carmel, an **affluent enclave** north of Indianapolis. This happened like five years ago, but Big City Nikki still scapegoats Columbus for some of her personal problems, most **particularly** her lack of a steady guy.

I hadn't even seen the dude yet, but already I was tempted to **abhor** this whole Luke **phenomenon**. I was thinking about how annoying it was that some stranger could penetrate the collective imagination of Columbus High more in one day than I had in the previous two years. And then, eight minutes into my last period class, AP English, in struts this tall, good-looking guy in paint-splattered jeans, a tight hipster T, and a shocking mass of curly reddish hair. Had to be him. *More* **intriguing** *than hot*, I thought. Of course, had I not been happily boyfriended to a legitimate hottie myself, I might have felt a little differently. There was something in his athletic **gait** that made you want to look. He had, like, star power. I made myself look away, determined not to fall victim to this **unabashed** "shock and awe" self-promotion campaign.

"You must be Lucas," Ms. Cloisters said.

"Luke," he said, apparently not the **verbose** type.

"Interesting," Ms. Cloisters said. "Do you know how I knew who you were, Luke?"

He shrugged.

"Well, it's not because your reputation **precedes** you, or that I received your dossier from the CIA. It's not because I saw you in the

---

ebullient: high-spirited
catalyst: something that brings about a change
affluent: wealthy

enclave: closed society
particularly: specifically
abhor: hate or detest
phenomenon: fact or event
intriguing: interesting

gait: way of walking
unabashed: unashamed
verbose: wordy
precedes: comes before

hallway and, admiring your **effulgent** beauty, rushed down to the principal's office to find out who you were." The class let out a few hesitant laughs. Ms. Cloisters had a reputation for humiliating students who didn't meet her **lofty** academic standards. "It was more along the lines that you were the last student to show. Why's that?"

"I'm new." Luke half-smiled in a way that said he'd played this game before. "I got lost."

"But you made it. You **persevered**. Congratulations, **neophyte**, on finding room 203. For future reference, the room numbers go in **descending** order from the opposite end of the hall. It's a logical scheme, and you're in Advanced Placement English, so you should be **cerebral** enough to figure it out. Now find a seat."

Luke turned his back on Ms. Cloisters, showing off his **stolid** expression to the rest of the class. I glanced up at him, prepared to **avert** my eyes at any moment. Didn't even score a glance. He sat behind me, in the same row. My back and shoulders felt warm. An **irrational** thought hit me—was he **emitting** some sort of Luke ray? I slumped down in my seat to fend it off.

Ms. Cloisters introduced the class with a **rant** about the power of words. Of the four things we would focus on in her class, vocabulary would be foremost. "It drives me nuts when students ask how studying words will ever assist them in the *real world*. The most bankable skill you could have in our media-driven society is to be **articulate**. In fact, a study conducted at several major corporations found that one of the most **salient disparities** between employees at the bottom-, middle-, and top-paying rungs is their skill levels in vocabulary and syntax. Which is to say, those who express themselves the best get the best jobs."

The final three things we would do in her class were read, read, and *read*. We would read Austen, Dostoevsky, Márquez, Plath, Hesse, and Hurston. We would read short stories, novels, novellas, poetry, epics, even a play. "In fact, we're going to start right now,"

---

effulgent: brilliant or radiant	**cerebral:** brainy or	**emitting:** giving off
lofty: superior	intelligent	**rant:** lecture
persevered: kept trying	**stolid:** indifferent	**articulate:** well-spoken
neophyte: beginner	**avert:** turn aside	**salient:** significant
descending: downward	**irrational:** not logical	**disparities:** differences

Ms. Cloisters said, handing out a short story by Hemingway for us to **peruse**.

It was called "Hills Like White Elephants," and it was about a young couple drinking beer in a bar, somewhere near some hills in Spain. It didn't seem like it had enough big words or concepts to be "good," but there was something to it, a certain **resonance**. Ms. Cloisters asked us what we thought about it. In **accordance** with my **resolution** to get more involved in class discussions this year, I raised my hand.

"Yes," Ms. Cloisters said. "Say your name, and then make your comment."

"My name's Francesca Castarelli. And I was just gonna say it seems like the couple in this story has some serious communication issues. They just talk in monosyllables about nothing in particular, and they can't seem to agree on anything."

"Okaaaay," Ms. Cloisters said in a **condescending** way. "Anyone else want to get a little more specific?" She pointed behind me.

"I'm Luke Barton, and I think the 'communication issues' Francesca is referring to are related to the fact that the young woman is pregnant with the man's child, and he is pressuring her to abort. That's what they're actually arguing about, even though they don't come right out and say it."

My ears got hot at the sound of my name. He was talking about me. Wait. Was he making fun of me? Was he calling me a **dunce**?

"That's right," Ms. Cloisters said. "Hemingway has a way of making a situation **implicit** without hitting the reader over the head with it. Nice close reading, Lucas."

Great. Humiliated by The New Guy. Maybe he hadn't meant to. I dropped my pencil and turned to steal a glance at him. Luke was looking back at me with a big ol' **smug** grin on his face. Jerk.

---

peruse: examine
resonance: character or tone

accordance: agreement
resolution: promise
condescending: degrading

dunce: idiot
implicit: implied
smug: self-satisfied

September 5: Read-a-Book Day

Okay, so maybe not much is different this year. But one thing I decided was that since I finally had a real boyfriend, I was going to enjoy that standard dating **ritual** that most girls my age have—a dinner-and-a-movie date. So far I had only experienced it **vicariously** through Nikki's stories and a dozen or so bad romantic comedies. I wanted it to be perfect, so I wore the most flatteringly functional outfit I could put together—tight jeans that showed off my soccer butt, a tank top with a lace trim that **embellished** my thin waist, a jade necklace that **complemented** my eyes, and a padded bra that flat-out lied about my (lack of) breasts.

The date started out great. When Jeremy picked me up, he pulled out flowers from behind his back—white lilies with backward-curving petals and little tongue-like tentacles bursting out of them. We'd been together for almost four months (counting the summer, which, to be fair, he was away for most of), and this was the first time he'd ever brought me flowers. Yeah, I totally swooned. Of course, such a romantic gesture clashed with my expectations about casual dinner-and-a-movie date **protocol**, but not enough to **inhibit** my full-on girly meltdown.

Dinner was at Red Lobster. After I recovered from seeing the tank of **forlorn** lobsters imprisoned near the entrance, their pinchers clamped together with rubber bands, I loosened up and enjoyed dinner. While we checked out our menus, the waitress brought us a basket full of **delectable** biscuits.

"Do these things have cheese in them?" I asked, still chewing.

---

ritual: tradition
vicariously: experience secondhand

embellished: decorated
complemented: matched
protocol: procedure

inhibit: restrain
forlorn: sad or dejected
delectable: tasty

"Yup," Jeremy said. "Aren't they good?"

"Mmm," I answered. "They're incredible. But, like, doesn't anyone realize that this kind of stuff is why this country has the fattest people in the world? I mean, we biggie-size our fries and inject mozzarella inside our pizza crusts, you know?"

"Huh?" he asked, his head still buried in the menu.

"Nothing."

"They taste great," he said, looking up. "And the reason we have the fattest people in the world is because no one exercises. We drive everywhere."

This had become a **tedious** habit of his—pretending not to hear a question, then answering it. Jeremy slapped his menu shut. The waitress came and gave us her Red Lobster shtick straight out of the training manual. He got the surf and turf. I got the tuna, medium rare. Then that thick, **immutable** silence that occurs after you order food set in. I nibbled on my cheese biscuit, doing a mental Google search under the topic: *things to say.*

"It's true," I said. "The **obese** ones are always the most **indolent**. But really, in terms of weight and fitness, America runs the whole **gamut**."

Jeremy tilted his head in confusion. "What on earth are you talking about?"

I tucked a strand of hair behind my ear. Chit-chat had never been my **forte**. "You know, it's like we have the lazy, fat people, but then we also have the other extreme, the **emaciated** supermodels and all the rich, yoga-vegan-superstars, people working like mad to be the best, to make more loot, more movies, more stuff."

Jeremy squinted. "Like Madonna?"

"Exactly," I said, **ecstatic** to have made the connection, any connection. I wanted to go for more, to let the conversation float upward into **abstraction** and **absurdity**, since I like nothing more than to **banter** about nothing in particular, but experience said to

---

tedious: dull or tiresome	**gamut:** spectrum	**abstraction:** formless
immutable: unchangeable	**forte:** strong point	concept
obese: very overweight	**emaciated:** very thin	**absurdity:** ridiculousness
indolent: lazy	**ecstatic:** overjoyed	**banter:** chit-chat

stop while I was ahead. I decided, instead, to check Jeremy out. I still hadn't gotten tired of just looking at him, taking in his cut jaw, big shoulders, hair gelled into an **unkempt** yet perfectly maintained mess. Hazel eyes. Long, curly eyelashes that gave him the lovable-yet-dopey look of the **innocuous** Joey from *Friends*.

"So have you met the new guy?" he asked.

This snapped me back into the world. I scrunched up my face, **feigning** ignorance. "Who?"

"The new dude. Jake Beachkin, or whatever."

"Oh . . ." I let out a giggle at that name. Sounded like a Barbie doll. He'd be Ken's snorkeling buddy, who came with a pair of butt-hugging, banana-hammock Speedo swim trunks and a pair of flippers. I cleared my throat and tried to be serious. "You mean Luke Barton?"

"Yeah," Jeremy said. "D'you meet him? What do you think?"

I waved the question away. "He's in my AP English class. Totally overrated."

"Really?"

"Yeah." I felt the **inexplicable** need to drive this point home more **tenaciously**. "From what I've seen, he's a **pompous** jerk."

"Strong words," Jeremy said.

"That's just my personal **assessment**. You can judge for yourself. Why do you ask, anyway?"

"Just wondering." Jeremy shrugged. But I could tell by how **apathetic** he was trying to be that something was **vexing** him. "I heard he's trying out for the team. He's a goalie too . . . Whatever. No big deal."

I hadn't figured out this whole girlfriend gig yet, but I assumed this was my cue. "Not that it will matter anyway," I said.

"Whattayamean?" he asked.

"Not that it will matter." I smiled. "Because you're better than him anyway."

---

unkempt: untidy	**inexplicable:** unexplainable	**assessment:** evaluation
innocuous: harmless	**tenaciously:** stubbornly	**apathetic:** uninterested
feigning: faking	**pompous:** pretentious, self-important	**vexing:** bothering

Jeremy smiled back. He cracked his knuckles. "That's right, baby."

The second half of our date, the movie part, didn't work out exactly as I'd planned. I was thinking air-conditioned cineplex; Jeremy pulled into the parking lot at Blockbuster. Since he'd paid for dinner and all, I kept quiet. But when he picked out the DVD for *2 Fast 2 Furious*, that stupid turbo-testosterone-fueled car-racing flick that, if I recall correctly, didn't get 2 many Oscar nominations, I decided to take a stand.

"Please no," I begged, pressing my hands together in the prayer position.

"But the first one was great," he said. "It's a great date movie."

I showed him the movie I had picked out, a foreign art-house film. "I've really been wanting to see this." I knew I had to do a better job of advertising. "The star is this beautiful French actress."

"Is it French?" Jeremy asked.

"Yeah."

"Subtitled?"

"I think so."

"No way."

I ground my teeth. Guys could be such **provincial** little puppies. "Okay, well if you insist upon seeing such a bad movie, can't we at least get some **maudlin** romantic trash . . . like something with Jennifer Lopez?"

"You girls and your emotional stuff. No way. We're getting *2 Fast 2 Furious*."

"Can't we check out the New Releases section?" I pleaded.

"Come on Francesca, don't you want to see this with me? I've been dying to rent it."

I tried several different types of persuasion—from **goading** to whining to sweet-talking—but he remained **obstinate**. I finally **capitulated**. We drove to his place and dodged his 'rents by parking down the block and slipping into the basement via the back door.

---

provincial: unsophisticated   **goading:** prodding   **capitulated:** surrendered
maudlin: sappy   **obstinate:** stubborn

Soon enough we were nice and snuggly on the plush maroon love seat that has witnessed roughly half of our hookup sessions, and I didn't mind so much that Jeremy hadn't wanted to go to a theater.

After a few dozen previews and a Pepsi commercial, the engines revved and the movie got started. It was just as bad as I'd figured it would be, but when I looked at Jeremy, his face was blue from the screen's reflection, eyes **transfixed** like a man possessed. *He doesn't even know I'm here.* I decided I should save him. Save him from being sucked into this . . . this quicksand pit of **vapidity**. I leaned in and started kissing his neck. *Now you know I'm here.* Jeremy pressed PAUSE on the remote. By the time he got the chance to unpause it, the screen was all snowy fuzz.

transfixed: spellbound   vapidity: lifelessness

September 13: National Peanut Day

Today was the first day of soccer tryouts. It's weird to be the captain and have to wear your game face all the time. Coach Haskins started out practice with some **rousing oration** about how we could be contenders for state this year. It would, however, take the kind of consistent focus and **discipline** shown last year by this year's captain, Francesca Castarelli. People clapped, and I got all aw-shucks and kicked at the dirt with my cleat.

"You probably have something you want to say to the girls, don't you?" Coach asked.

I **blanched**. "Something to say?"

"Yes. You know, a motivational speech for the players fighting for a spot."

I hated setups like that. It was like when someone said how funny your joke was, right before you told it—always killed it. "A speech, right . . . the thing is, my favorite tradition on this team is the warm-up run, so I was hoping to get to know the girls while we run. To show them that I not only talk the talk . . . but jog the jog."

Coach agreed it was a good idea. In my most commandingly alpha male voice, I told everyone to get off their butts and follow me. They did. It had been a full-fledged tsunami all day until right before school let out, so it was like trudging through marshlands.

"For those of you who are returning to the girls' varsity team," I said, loud enough for Coach to hear. "You know that the most fun we have is after the games we've won. But to get to those celebrations, especially the big ones at the end of the season, we have to

---

rousing: inspiring
oration: speech

discipline: self-control

blanched: went pale

make it through weeks of wind sprints and lung-heaving, hard-working, tough-tackling G.I. Jane–style pract—"

"Fran," a voice to my right said. "You can stop. She's not watching."

"Oh," I said, already **foreseeing** the slip in my **credibility** as captain.

"Can we run over past the boys' field?" someone asked.

"How about this," I said. "We'll stop right here and count out a set of fifty jumping jacks. Then I'll score some points for being tough, and we can run over there without risking Coach Haskin's **wrath**. Deal?"

We did our fifty jacks, even **relishing** the out-loud counting for its wink-wink, **covert** mission element. Of course, this **diplomacy** was part of a larger psychological **ploy** on my part to win the hearts and minds of my teammates. It was the old foot-in-the-door **ruse**. Once I establish myself as one of them, I have paved the way to becoming their **intrepid** leader.

"Okay, let's run behind the goal," I said. "And pick up the pace, so we don't look too **conspicuous**."

I lengthened my strides and listened with satisfaction to the **euphonious** patter of running feet behind me. I had always dug this part of team sports—a group of people moving in **unison** toward a common goal. In this case, our rather **ignoble** short-term goal was to watch cute boys run around in shorts.

"Kyle Yaeger is so yummy," someone said.

"He's looking over here . . ."

A **din** of chatter escalated—the sound of friction between guys and girls checking each other out. As we ran behind the goal, I finally spotted the one I'd been looking for. My guy. Or, I should say, my guy's better half.

"Hey goalie," I yelled out. "Nice butt!"

Waves of laughter **erupted** behind me. I congratulated myself. Not only was I their **dauntless** leader but witty to boot, and with

foreseeing: predicting
credibility: trustworthiness
wrath: anger
relishing: savoring
covert: secret
diplomacy: skillful negotiation

ploy: tactic or strategy
ruse: trick
intrepid: fearless
conspicuous: noticeable
euphonious: pleasant sounding

unison: harmony
ignoble: dishonorable
din: clamor or noise
erupted: burst forth
dauntless: fearless

a cute goalie for a boyfriend. He turned around in a molasses-slow way that struck me as **surreal**. *Uh oh,* I thought, his smiling face registering in my mind. *That butt doesn't belong to my boyfriend.* My teammates let out a collective gasp. *That butt belongs to that face.* I broke into a half-sprint at the **revelation**. *And that face belongs to Luke Barton.*

surreal: unreal or strange   **revelation:** realization

September 20: Oktoberfest Begins (Germany)

Nikki and I went to "study" tonight at the library. Columbus has the sickest library you've ever seen. It's this big, **cavernous** lump of red bricks and glass, and the interior is straight off the Sci Fi Channel. It was designed by I. M. Pei. He's a Chinese guy who is, as far as I know, The World's Coolest Library Maker.

I put quotation marks around "study" because it's impossible to be **diligent** with Nikki around. She's too damn **loquacious**. I call her Miss Quack Quack when she gets like this.

"I mean, the problem is, now that this skateboarding magazine that features him is out there, he's become a total celebrity. Luke Barton, pro skateboarder! I actually saw him get groped in the hallway today. I can already see him starring in some extreme-sports-themed version of a cheesy hip-hop video, with a **bevy** of smiling half-naked sophomores **dousing** his silk boxers with champagne. It's just like me to fall for a rock star at the **apex** of his career, you know?"

"Yeah," I said.

"I mean, the kid could run for mayor. It totally sucks. At this point, if a **prominent** senior hottie steps to Luke, I don't have a snowball's chance in you know where." She looked down and shook her head, all **distraught**.

"Shhh," a faceless voice from the other side of the garden said. Nikki made a "talk to the hand" motion in the direction it came from.

"But Nikki, you *like* challenges," I said, giving her a **maternal**

---

cavernous: huge and empty
diligent: hard working
loquacious: talkative

bevy: crowd
dousing: drenching
apex: height

prominent: well-known
distraught: upset
maternal: motherly

pat on the leg. "You like guys who are hard to get. That's one of the things we love about you."

"That's true. And I know I can land him. I'm not worried. Hey, you wanna look at the magazine again?"

"Please no," I begged. "Not again."

But it was too late. From her backpack, Nikki pulled out a tattered copy of *SK8R* magazine. She turned to the dog-eared page. "Just look at him," she said, tilting the magazine for me to **scrutinize** his photo, *once again*. I had to admit, he was more appealing—**aesthetically** at least—on paper than he was in reality.

"He's like an angel on wheels," she said, dreamily. "A flying **cherub**."

"Well if you're so gaga over him, why don't you just throw yourself at him?" I asked.

"No! Don't you see? That's exactly what I *can't* do. I have to be **subtle**, so I stand out from all his groupies. I can't just slink up to his locker, batting my eyelashes and showing off my cleavage like a skank. I need time and space for him to notice me. I mean, my problem is . . . what I'm missing is . . ."

"A chromosome?" I suggested.

"What? No. I'm missing that thing where you happen to end up at the same party with the right guy because you know the same people through six degrees of separation. You know what I mean?"

"You mean **context**," I said **authoritatively**.

"Exactly! Context. I mean, I don't have a single class with Luke. Even you, you have AP English. You play on the soccer team. You probably see him some out at the fields, in those short shorts."

"Not really." For some reason, I had been too **abashed** to tell Nikki about the *"hey goalie, nice butt"* incident with Luke. "The boys' and girls' teams don't mix much."

"Well, I need to get some Luke context somehow."

"Force it," I said.

---

scrutinize: examine closely
aesthetically: relating to beauty

cherub: angel
subtle: understated
context: setting

authoritatively: with command
abashed: embarrassed

"What?"

"Force it," I said. "*Create* the context."

She **ruminated** on that for a second, then shot me a confused look. "What's that supposed to mean? Are you saying I should start a skateboarding club or something?"

"You don't skateboard," I said. "That would make you a hard-core tool."

"Ahem," a voice interrupted.

We both looked up. It was Eric Crowther. He's **essentially** a prep/hood hybrid. Too **erudite** and well-off to be a card-carrying hood, but too stoned and **sartorially** handicapped to be a prep. At the end of sophomore year, after I had a major growth spurt that led to an **accretion** of five inches, four guys decided at once that I was no longer "compact" but "hot." Eric was one of those four suitors from the now-famous Francesca Bidding War, which boosted my social status at Columbus High. Eric lost the auction, of course, to Jeremy, for reasons no more **substantive** than Nikki's claim that Jeremy was the "highest draft pick." Now Eric stood above us, his pale blue eyes at half-mast, his expression **stoic**.

"Why is it . . ." he asked, stroking an imaginary goatee, "that some people go to the library to talk?"

It seemed like a **rhetorical** question. We didn't answer. Eric shook his head and walked away.

---

ruminated: thought about
essentially: basically
erudite: scholarly

sartorially: style of dress
accretion: increase
substantive: real or solid

stoic: stone-faced
rhetorical: asked for effect

September 26: National Good Neighbor Day

Lunchtime. Taco Bell.

Nikki and I have last lunch period, so the dining area was **rife** with taco wrappers and used hot sauce packets. I sat in our favorite booth, next to the window least **obscured** by those huge Taco Bell sticker ads, waiting for Nikki to bring the food over. She had **magnanimously** offered to pay for the food and deliver it to our table. This type of unprompted **altruism** was so **atypical** of Nikki that I was, quite frankly, suspicious.

"Here you go," Nikki said, carrying a tray like a waitress. "A chicken gordita, Mexican pizza, burrito, and a Coke."

"Thanks."

"No problem!" Nikki said, a little too ecstatically. "I'm just so pumped we have the same lunch period."

"Yeah. Pretty cool." We'd had the same lunch period for weeks now. Why she chose this moment to **revel** in that long-gone stroke of **serendipity** was a flat-out **conundrum** to me.

"Isn't it gorgeous out?" Nikki said, looking outside. "God, what a day!"

I stared at her, **dumbfounded**. This was exactly the type of **saccharine**, glass-half-full **optimism** we had always mutually **railed** against. The first time Nikki and I met was at a CH football game, when she overheard me verbally shredding the cheerleaders for looking like **pliable** plastic dolls. She cackled out loud, and I cackled back, and our cackles **reverberated** throughout the bleachers, and we've been *us* ever since.

---

rife: filled
obscured: covered
magnanimously: generously
altruism: self-sacrifice
atypical: out of character
revel: enjoy

serendipity: luck
conundrum: puzzle, riddle
dumbfounded: astonished
saccharine: overly sweet

optimism: cheerfulness
railed: ranted
pliable: bendable
reverberated: echoed

"Pintos 'n Cheese is the nectar of the gods. So good." Nikki was chewing with her eyes closed.

"I'm not gonna argue there." I finished chomping my gordita and leaned into the table. "But that alone would not explain your suddenly **metamorphosing** into the Bartholomew County Teen Spirit Queen. Would it?"

Nikki shrugged, smiled, and jabbed her spork into what looked like cheese-covered mud. She shoveled it into her mouth with **exuberance**.

"Come on," I **exhorted**. "Spill the beans."

She almost snorted up a mouthful of mush. "That was the worst joke ever, Fran . . . Okay, okay, so I was saving it for dessert, but I guess I'll tell you. I talked to him today."

"Him? You mean Luke?"

"Yeah."

"So you figured out a context?"

"I did," she said. "Thanks for the advice."

"Wow. So how'd it go?"

"Oh, my God. It was incredible. We totally established **rapport**. There's just something about that guy—he's got that quiet simmering brain-power thing. He observes everything but doesn't comment too much."

"He's **succinct**," I said.

"Totally. And he stays kind of withdrawn and makes you come after him, you know."

"So he's **elusive**," I said.

"Are you kidding me? Totally. He's everything. He's like the *un*-gettable guy."

"Your ideal mate," I said, slurping at my straw **disdainfully**.

"Exactly."

"So how did you do it?" I asked.

"Do what?"

---

metamorphosing: changing   **rapport:** mutual   **elusive:** hard to pin down
exuberance: enthusiasm   understanding   **disdainfully:** scornfully
exhorted: urged   **succinct:** brief

"Create context."

"Oh. Well. I . . ." Nikki put her spork down. She wiped Taco Bell residue from her hands with a napkin. Not in a normal, massaging motion but more **akin** to the **deranged**, obsessive-compulsive Lady Macbeth manner of hand rubbing.

"You what?" I prodded.

"Well what happened was, I remembered—total **coincidence** here—that you weren't so **enthralled** with your writing PSAT scores. And I heard that Luke is a seriously smart guy, with a huge vocabulary, so I figured, hey, we could kill three birds with one stone or whatever. You know . . . help me, help you, help him. It's a win-win win situation . . ."

"Excuse me Nikki," I said. "How exactly did *I* get involved here?"

Nikki ran her hand over her hair, and I noticed that her hand was **quivering**. "I signed you up for vocab tutoring lessons with Luke. Just like once every couple weeks."

"You did *what?*"

"Think of it as an early birthday gift for my best friend," she said.

I stabbed my spork **vehemently** into my Mexican pizza. "My birthday is a month away. And why would I want tutoring lessons from a guy I **detest**, especially in vocabulary, when you know that I pride myself on my verbal **legerdemain?**"

"Yeah, yeah, I know. You're good with words. But I figured that since you scored way lower than you should have that—"

"Be nice," I said.

"Oh, I know. I'm so sorry. I know I'm psycho. Go ahead and take me away in a straitjacket . . ." Nikki slumped down in the booth. "It's just that, you told me to establish context, and I brainstormed all night, and that was all I could come up with."

"Why didn't you at least ask me first?"

"You would have said no."

"**Valid** point. But then—why didn't you just get lessons for

akin: similar	**quivering:** trembling	**legerdemain:** sleight of
deranged: crazy	**vehemently:** forcefully	hand
coincidence: pure chance	**detest:** strongly dislike	**valid:** truthful, accurate
enthralled: enchanted		

yourself? Why for me? How is my getting lessons from him going to help your cause at all?"

"I don't know." She groaned. "I don't want him to think I'm dumb, especially when I practically needed a dictionary just to carry on a conversation with him. It just seemed too **blatant**. I didn't want to put myself, you know, *below* him from the very beginning of the relationship. I figure this way I can get to know him slowly, through you, and strike that perfect balance between accessible and right there in your face, you know?"

"Sweet. So now I get to be **illiterate** for you, by **proxy**."

Nikki nodded. "I guess you could put it that way. I'm so sorry. I know I'm a bad person . . . **deplorable** scum, a **wretched** low-life . . ." She scooched out of the booth and got on her knees, next to me. She clasped her hands together and shot me puppy-dog eyes. "I confess my sins. But please, if you have any **empathy** for me what-soever, you'll take these lessons. I'm paying for them, and you know how **frugal** I can be . . ."

"Gee," I said. "Thanks for your **patronage**."

"Pleeeeeeeeeeease," she begged. I almost pitied the girl. Unbe-lievable what we're willing to do for the opposite sex.

"But I don't need vocab lessons," I said. "What am I sup-posed to do, pretend I'm a moron so he doesn't catch on to our **machinations**?"

"That would be nice."

"I don't know," I said, though I could feel myself softening some-what. "I think I need some more **incentive**."

"You want another Mexican Pizza?" she asked hopefully.

"No," I answered, holding out for a better contract. "But some-thing. I don't know. We'll see . . ."

blatant: obvious	**deplorable:** terrible	**patronage:** monetary
illiterate: uneducated	**wretched:** miserable	support
proxy: substitution	**empathy:** compassion	**machinations:** schemes
	frugal: thrifty	**incentive:** motivation

October 1: Chinese Moon Festival

After she bribed me with a gift certificate for a free massage, I finally **acquiesced** to Nikki's demands. Which is why, after soccer practice today, she dropped me off in Forest Estates at 3224 Grove Parkway—aka, the House o' Luke. We could barely see the house number because of all the trees and vines and **fecund** greenery **cascading** onto his front lawn.

"This is like a freakin' rain forest," Nikki said.

"Well, if I get **assassinated** by some **irate** primate, it'll be on your **conscience**."

"You'll be fine," Nikki said. "Thank you so much for doing this. You're the greatest."

"No prob. Anything for a friend and a deep tissue massage." I smiled. "By the way, what's your plan? Are you gonna wait until he answers the door and then just jump out and **accost** him?"

"What am I, an idiot? Wait—don't answer that," she said quickly when she saw the smile on my face. "I don't know, I may wave or something. I haven't decided whether to make my move today. Feeling kind of blah. I was thinking I'd let you get to know him a little first, and then give me some hints about the best way to reel him in."

"Got it," I said.

I stepped out of the car. The full **import** of what I was about to do occurred to me for the first time. *Getting tutored by an* **egomaniac** *I don't know so that Nikki can score a boyfriend.* I shuffled across the lawn and pressed the doorbell. After an **interminable** silence,

acquiesced: agreed	**irate:** angry	**egomaniac:** self-centered
fecund: fertile	**conscience:** moral sense	person
cascading: pouring	**accost:** approach	**interminable:** endless
assassinated: killed	**import:** meaning	

there was the tap-tap of footsteps on tile. The door creaked open. I held my already **bated** breath. A face appeared, but not Luke's. It was the softened face of a **matriarch** who, despite her graying hair, maintained the **radiant** smile and general **vivacity** of a much younger woman.

"Hello," she said. "You must be Francesca."

"That's me."

"Nice to meet you. I'm Mrs. Barton," she said with a **genial** smile. She extended her hand. I shook it. "Welcome to our humble **abode**."

"Thanks."

She gestured for me to step inside. The house smelled like cinnamon and **desiccated** lemon peels. I heard the **mellifluous** sprinkle of running water in the background.

"Would your friend like to come in too?" she asked, gesturing behind me.

"Oh . . ." I turned around and shooed Nikki away with a **dismissive** flick of the wrist. "No. She dropped me off. She's leaving. Thanks."

"Luke got home late from practice. He's still in the shower. Can I get you something to drink?"

"No thanks," I said **bashfully**, even though I was a little thirsty.

Mrs. Barton and I **prattled** for a bit about how nice a town Columbus was. She apologized **extensively** for her son's **tardiness** and then asked me to excuse her. She was a therapist and had lots of paperwork to do.

I said no problem. I waited there, alone, in the den, listening to the shower run, for a solid five minutes. Which may not seem like a long time, but it is when the person who is supposed to be tutoring you is **flippantly** whistling to himself in a shower just a few feet away. I could feel the anger **amassing** inside me, and I knew that I would have to **suppress** it somehow in order to maintain my **civility**.

---

bated: restrained
matriarch: ruling female
radiant: glowing
vivacity: liveliness
genial: friendly
abode: home

desiccated: dried out
mellifluous: smooth-sounding
dismissive: haughty
bashfully: shyly
prattled: chatted

extensively: in-depth
tardiness: lateness
flippantly: disrespectfully
amassing: collecting
suppress: stifle
civility: politeness

I realized the shower had stopped and **poised** myself for His Highness to step out and finally **grace** me with his presence. The door opened.

"Oh hey," he said **unassumingly**. "You're on time. So **punctual**. I'm sorry. You must think I'm such a punk."

I didn't say anything. He stood there, his freckled skin **flecked** with glistening beads of water, holding up his towel at the waist. I swallowed hard. He was lankier than I expected him to be, more **sinewy** than buff. I indulged in a shallow thought: *Jeremy's got a tighter six-pack.* I wanted him to know I was annoyed without having to say it. I wanted badly to feign **disinterest**, just as I had planned, but he was suddenly too human, too *right there*. It was **disarming**.

"No problem," I heard myself saying.

"Listen, I'll go throw on some clothes and grab my stuff. Be right back . . ." He started to walk away, and I couldn't help watching. When he flipped around, he caught me in a compromising position. "And don't be checkin' out my butt," he said.

I bit my lip, feeling my face turn five different shades of red.

But when he came back, Luke immediately got down to business. I was stunned at how professional and, quite frankly, how good he was at tutoring. I was less **beset** by **ennui** than I'd imagined I'd be. At the same time, it was clear that he **grossly** underestimated my verbal **acumen**, which annoyed me. But I sucked it up and played ignoramus in the name of **allegiance** to Nikki. My **aplomb** held up for almost the full hour, until, with about ten minutes left, he corrected my pronunciation of the word "**arduous**."

"It's not *are-joo-us*," he said. "Technically, you're supposed to pronounce the 'd.' More like, *are-dyoo-us*."

I threw my hands up in the air. "Listen, I know the word, all right. I know that it means 'involving great difficulty or effort,' and I've heard it pronounced **myriad** times, by teachers, parents, and

poised: composed	**disinterest**: lack of concern	**allegiance**: loyalty
grace: honor	**disarming**: charming	**aplomb**: poise
unassumingly: modestly	**beset**: troubled, harassed	**arduous**: difficult
punctual: on time	**ennui**: boredom	**myriad**: numerous
flecked: speckled	**grossly**: hugely	
sinewy: lean	**acumen**: intelligence	

newscasters, and I know that my pronunciation is just as legitimate as yours."

"Whoa," he said. "Easy there. I'm just trying to help out."

"Well, you're not." I popped the cap on my pen for emphasis. "See, I'm afraid I've misled you somewhat. My friend signed me up for this because—um, because she heard me complain about my PSAT score from last year. But I've come a long way since then, and I don't really need this tutoring. In fact, from what I've seen, my vocabulary **prowess** is basically **tantamount** to yours."

"I doubt that, considering I've taken several SAT prep classes."

"All the more reason for me to conserve time, energy, and money by **renouncing** this little charade and going back to the vocab workbooks I've already bought."

"Oh, so you *are* trying to **bolster** your score then?"

"I didn't say that."

"Well, if you are, then trust me, no exercise could be more **otiose** than laboring over those workbooks without an actual person to help you out."

Otiose? What the . . . ?

"It means **futile**." Luke grinned at his own **clairvoyance**.

"I know what it means," I lied.

Luke put up his hands in **mock** surrender. "Fine. I believe you. Listen, today I'm going to give you the **abridged** lesson. And from now on, I'll **concede** that you're an advanced student. Instead of doing these **mundane** exercises, we'll just do **random** free-style word-offs, using **bombastic** words in discussions and **polemics**, just to amuse ourselves. We'll both get better scores, and my parents can keep **deluding** themselves that I'm a responsible, **industrious** young adult with an actual income from this tutoring gig. How's that sound?"

I paused, debating. This whole afternoon had been a waste of time, mostly. But I *had* picked up a few words I didn't know, and I

prowess: skill	clairvoyance:	random: patternless
tantamount: equal	perceptiveness	bombastic: pompous
renouncing: rejecting	mock: fake	polemics: arguments
bolster: strengthen	abridged: shortened	deluding: deceiving
otiose: useless	concede: grant	industrious: hard-working
futile: pointless	mundane: ordinary	

knew Nikki would freak out if I told her the whole plan was over before she'd even had a chance to take action.

"Sounds okay," I said, trying to keep my tone from sounding as sulky as I felt.

"You know, I have to say that you deserve some **plaudits** yourself. From my first impression, I **presumed** you were totally regs."

"Regs?"

"Yeah, you know. Normal. Dull. Plain Jane. A carbon copy embracer of the status quo . . ."

"I get your point."

"But I'm not so sure about you anymore. You've got some guts."

"Coo, thanks," I said. Nothing **infuriated** me more than a back-handed **compliment**.

Luke stood up. "Cool. So, I'll see you next time," he said with cool self-assurance.

---

plaudits: applause   **infuriated:** angered   **compliment:** flattering
presumed: supposed   remark

"You thought it was *my* butt?" Jeremy complained. "How's that possible? How could we be dating for this long and you can't **distinguish** mine from someone else's?"

"I don't know!" I said. "We were running. I couldn't see!"

This was the umpteenth time our conversation had returned to The Incident. We were ambling through Fair Oaks Mall. The search for a present for Jeremy's niece had somehow turned into me desperately trying to **mollify** Jeremy's annoyance. As I probably should have expected, an **eavesdropping** fullback overheard my comment to Luke, and it had found its way back to Jeremy. Now he was being so **querulous** about the topic, I was starting to wonder if I'd accidentally **exhumed** some **latent** insecurity Jeremy had about his butt.

"But you have perfect vision." He shook his head. "It just doesn't add up."

"What can I say? I'm human. I'm **fallible**. I'm sorry."

"It's just so stupid, Fran. I mean, why would you yell out *nice butt* even if you thought it *was* me? It's not like I would've been all psyched, like, *Yeah. That's my girlfriend.*"

"All right, listen," I said. "I get your point. I don't know what I was thinking, okay? Now, can we put a **moratorium** on this topic? Because we've reached an **impasse**, and I can't just keep apologizing over and over."

Jeremy dropped my hand. "And that's another thing. You're always trying to use big words. You sound all **stilted**, like . . ." Jeremy

distinguish: tell between	**querulous:** argumentative	**moratorium:** an end
mollify: subdue	**exhumed:** dug up	**impasse:** standstill
eavesdropping: snooping or listening in	**latent:** hidden	**stilted:** stiff
	fallible: imperfect	

bobbled his head and spoke in a nasally voice, **mimicking** me. "I've noticed your **penchant** for verbosity and have decided to put a moratoriad on your speaking . . ."

"A mora-*what?*" I asked.

"Forget it. You know what I mean. Why can't you just talk like a normal person?"

I was about to snap back something about how he should really be working on his own vocabulary anyway, when I saw the hurt look in his eyes and realized this wasn't the time. Jeremy's ego had suffered a real bruising, and what he needed now was some serious smoothing over, not just more fighting.

"Let's check out this store," I said, grabbing his elbow and steering him inside. It was one of those gift stores where everything was either a gag gift or a **parody** of some actual gift.

"How about this?" I said, picking up a box. "You think little Claire would like some edible underwear?"

"Ewww," Jeremy said. "That's gross."

"Yeah, I'm thinking this isn't really the place to find a present for your three-year-old niece."

"I just wish the guys on the team hadn't heard," Jeremy muttered. Apparently my attempt at distraction hadn't worked. "What really bugs me is that now they all think my girlfriend wants that stupid **poseur**. And you don't even know the guy."

"Well, actually—" I froze, clamping my mouth shut before I could say another word.

Okay, I know, it's big-time wrong to lie to your boyfriend. But is it still a lie if you just, like, leave something out? Because right as I was about to tell Jeremy how Luke was tutoring me, I realized that it would be just about the last thing he'd want to hear. The timing was all wrong.

"Actually, what?" Jeremy asked, his expression wary.

I smoothed my skirt to steady myself. "Oh, nothing—I was just

---

mimicking: imitating   **parody:** spoof   **poseur:** pretender
penchant: fondness

going to say you shouldn't care what those guys think," I said. It was totally lame, but it seemed to work, because the suspicious look in his eyes faded back to the scowl that had been there a second ago.

"You just don't get what it's like," he said. "Guys are different."

"I know. I'm sorry," I said, giving him my best wide-eyed adoring girlfriend half-smile. "But it's over, okay? And I just had an idea—we should check out *That's Pretty Personal*. It's a few doors down, and I think you'll find something there."

Jeremy followed me to the store, and his mood eased when he caught sight of the display window. "This store looks perfect."

"I told you. It's got really unique gifts."

A woman approached us as soon as we walked in. She was smiling so **solicitously** that you knew she had to work there. "Can I help you two?" she asked.

"We're looking for a gift," I said.

"For a little girl," Jeremy added.

"How old is she?" the woman asked.

"Three."

"Birthday?" she **inquired**.

"Uh huh," Jeremy said.

"Follow me," she said. "I think I have the perfect thing. Have you ever seen Groovy Girls? All little girls love Groovy Girls."

She led us to the back of the store, and Jeremy forgot all about Luke as I helped him choose which Groovy Girl Claire would like best.

I'm not going to say there wasn't a little twinge hanging around my stomach, reminding me that it wasn't such a good idea to keep quiet about the tutoring thing. But I'm not going to be doing this stupid tutoring thing much longer anyway. Once Nikki reels Luke in, I'll be out of there. Jeremy will never have to know.

Ignorance is, as the **maxim** goes, **bliss**.

---

solicitously: kindly   maxim: saying   bliss: delight
inquired: asked

October 22: National Nut Day

Tonight was opening night for varsity soccer. There's nothing like that **anticipation**, that nervous churning in your gut as you lace up your cleats. We trotted out of the locker room, me leading my **troupe** of soccer warriors. A faint **zephyr** blew across the field, **disseminating** the aroma of freshly mowed grass. We were greeted by loud cheers from the **obstreperous** crowd of rabble-rousing fans that Columbus High is **infamous** for.

The game was tight. This year I'm playing center halfback, which means I'm responsible for setting up most of our plays, both offensive and defensive. Coach says I'm supposed to be **indefatigable** in pursuit of the ball but never lose my **composure**. I thought I did a decent job of that throughout the first half. But in the second half, with the game deadlocked in a 0-0 **stalemate**, **fatigue** set in and I started to get **flustered**. The girl who was defending me—this total Amazon chick—kept grabbing the back of my jersey when the ref wasn't looking. Fed up with her **mendacious** strategy, and the fact that I was getting no whistles, I jogged up and asked the ref about her vision problems. "What are you, **myopic**?"

She blew the whistle and gave me a yellow card. I deserved it, I guess. The crowd stood behind me though, heckling the officials with the chant: "Three blind mice! Three blind mice!"

In the last few minutes of the game, my dogged **persistence** paid off. Someone passed me the ball in front of the goal, and when I turned to shoot, Amazon Chick hacked me. The ref blew the whistle. Penalty kick. Coach yelled out for Natalie Gaskill to take it,

---

anticipation: state of expectation
troupe: group
zephyr: breeze
disseminating: spreading

obstreperous: hostile
infamous: well-known
indefatigable: tireless
composure: self-control
stalemate: standoff

fatigue: exhaustion
flustered: upset, confused
mendacious: dishonest
myopic: short-sighted
persistence: endurance

since her shot was the most **accurate**. **Emboldened** by the rush of adrenaline that I always feel in the face of injustice, I **dissented**.

"Let me take it," I told Coach, with utter **certitude**. "I'll make it."

"It's all you then," Coach said.

As I walked toward the penalty stripe, an **intimidating** hush fell over the crowd. *Focus, Francesca.* I noticed that a group of guys had assembled behind the goal. It was the guys' varsity team, who had a game right after us. *Focus. Don't look.* But it was too late. I saw Jeremy first. He clenched his fist in **solidarity** and nodded as if to say: *You got it, babe.* I glanced to the left of him, and there, smiling a huge, **beatific** smile, was Luke.

I closed my eyes and tried to block them out. *Visualize the ball going into the net.* I set the ball down. The goalie was hunched over and glaring at me. *Focus.* I took a few steps back, exhaled, and charged at the ball. But at the last second, something went **awry**. I kicked down the middle, right into the goalie's chest. Worst shot ever. Luckily, she bobbled it. I pounced on the rebound and scored. It wasn't pretty, but a goal was a goal. The crowd roared. My teammates surrounded me. I was a heroine, for the moment at least.

After our game, I showered and went out to cheer Jeremy on. Before I got to the bleachers, I saw Nikki running toward me. I assumed she wanted to give me **kudos** for a job well done, but the distressed look on her face suggested otherwise.

"What's up?" I asked.

"It's Jeremy," she said. "He came down hard on his ankle, first save of the game. His parents just drove him to the hospital."

accurate: precise	**certitude:** assurance	**beatific:** saintly
emboldened: encouraged	**intimidating:** frightening	**awry:** out of kilter, wrong
dissented: disagreed	**solidarity:** unity	**kudos:** praise, applause

October 23:
My Birthday

Talk about bad timing—can you believe I had to have my seventeenth birthday today, right after Jeremy's injury? I guess I should have been prepared for disappointment, considering how **grim** my horoscope was. Here's an **excerpt**: "Dear **obdurate** and controlling Scorpio, Unless you surrender to those circumstances beyond your control, you could end up in the eye of the storm. Proceed with caution. Little quirks may surface in a new relationship (personal or work), leaving you to rethink the depth of your commitment." Hmmm . . .

The day wasn't a complete loss, I guess. Nikki got me a cool shirt and some sunglasses from Urban Outfitters in Indy. My parents made me a steak dinner and a cake. After that, I went over to Jeremy's to fulfill my duty as **doting** girlfriend. I couldn't even really enjoy my day until then, because I was so anxious to make sure he was okay.

So, he's going to be fine, but it turns out he sprained his ankle, so he's going to be out for the rest of the season. I felt terrible for him, but the thing is, it was still my birthday, you know? And I hate to **wallow** in self-pity, but I couldn't believe Jeremy didn't even get me a present. He gave me a card and apologized **elaborately** for being too **incapacitated** to go shopping, but that wasn't enough to make **amends**. Especially since all he could talk about was one thing. Or, actually, one person . . .

"I can't believe, after how hard I trained this summer." Jeremy bared his teeth. "I mean, did you see how bad his technique was?

grim: dismal	**doting:** devoted	**incapacitated:** unable
excerpt: brief passage	**wallow:** roll around	**amends:** apologies
obdurate: hard-hearted	**elaborately:** with great care, at length	

Did you see the way he flopped around like a fish?"

"Who's that?" I asked, playing dumb.

"Luke!" he yelled. "Did you see how mediocre he was?"

Didn't look so bad to me, I thought. *I noticed he didn't get scored on.* I immediately felt guilty for thinking that, but Jeremy's self-absorption was getting on my nerves.

"Did you notice?" Jeremy prodded.

"I wasn't paying attention," I said.

"Oh." Jeremy looked back up at the TV. "Well, he sucked."

Sweet, I thought. *Happy birthday to me.*

October 27: Mother-in-Law's Day

I had my second tutorial with Luke today. Having listened to a week-long stream of **vitriol** from Jeremy about the chump who **usurped** his spot on the team, I couldn't help but feel **combative** toward Luke. Instead of **reciprocating** my chilly **demeanor**, though, Luke responded by being gentlemanly and sweet.

"How's your boyfriend feeling?" he asked.

"Okay." I figured **concise** replies would discourage any further **interrogation**.

"That sucks for him, man. Ankle injuries are the worst."

"Yeah."

"So how long have you two been going out?"

"Four months."

"Oh yeah? Did you have a crush on him before that?" he asked, giving me a teasing grin.

"Not really," I said **curtly**. "I thought we were supposed to be doing vocab stuff."

"Oh right. My bad." He shuffled through his papers and handed me a **catalog** of words. "Here. How about we just try having a conversation using the words on this sheet?"

"Sure," I said. "You start."

Luke cleared his throat. "**Hypothetically**, it's best for a newcomer to fully **immerse** himself in his new **environs**."

I squinted at the page, trying to assemble a thought. "Unless, of course, the new environs are **fraught** with freaks who throw themselves **ignominiously** at the newcomer."

vitriol: rage	demeanor: manner	hypothetically: theoretically
usurped: seized	concise: brief	immerse: plunge
combative: argumentative	interrogation: questioning	environs: surroundings
reciprocating: returning	curtly: tersely	fraught: filled
	catalog: directory	ignominiously: shamefully

"In which case, he should **recoil** from those **noxious** creatures, into his own **realm**."

I gave Luke a look. "Which assumes, perhaps **erroneously**, that our newcomer is male." He laughed. "In which case," I added. "*He* should be **wary** not to **ostracize** himself, to keep from turning himself into a **pariah**."

"Perhaps, though," Luke responded, "if he finds a woman worthy of his **idolatry**—the very **paragon** of grace and beauty—and if she arouses within him deep **pathos**, he will be too **preoccupied** to care that he's a pariah."

I looked at him. There was something **coquettish** to his tone, but I couldn't **decipher** the meaning of what he'd said through the thick **morass** of needlessly big words.

"But where would one find such a babe?" I asked. "A creature so **incredible** that she made all other females seem bland and **superfluous**."

"He may not have to look far."

"No vocab words," I said. "You lose."

We did a few more exercises, then played Boggle for the rest of the **allotted** time. When the session was over, I asked Luke about one of the plants in his **verdant** front lawn as a **guise** to get him to escort me outside. We were barely out the door when I saw Nikki strutting toward us, using the lawn as a runway to show off a mighty scant outfit.

"Hey!" I said, stretching my acting skills to the utmost. "How **opportune**. We just finished. Luke, I think you remember my friend Nikki, the benefactor for our tutoring sessions."

"Of course."

"So how was he?" Nikki asked in her **sultriest** tone. "Is he as good a wordsmith as he claims to be?"

I looked at Luke, raising my eyebrows. I wasn't about to give his superinflated ego any extra stroking.

---

recoil: withdraw	**idolatry:** worship	**incredible:** extraordinary
noxious: toxic	**paragon:** ideal	**superfluous:** unnecessary
realm: territory	**pathos:** pity	**allotted:** prearranged
erroneously: wrongly	**preoccupied:** lost in thought	**verdant:** green
wary: cautious	**coquettish:** flirtatious	**guise:** excuse
ostracize: exile	**decipher:** decode	**opportune:** timely
pariah: outsider	**morass:** tangle	**sultriest:** steamiest

But it didn't seem to matter, anyway. Luke wasn't even paying attention to me. His eyes were glued to Nikki, and judging from the way he was **ogling** her, even the great Luke Barton was **mortal**. His mild amusement for our silly word games was **immaterial** in comparison. Whatever electrostatic current Nikki and Luke were volleying back and forth didn't involve me. I was definitely **extraneous** here. "Is your cell phone in your car?" I asked. "I need to call my mom."

"Oh," Nikki said, not even looking at me. "Yeah. It's in the car. Back seat."

I sat in the car with the radio on, pretending to call mom but fully absorbed in watching them. It's weird to witness raw, chemical attraction. I know I should have been relieved to see the way they were flirting with each other. It meant Nikki's plan was already working, and I was one step closer to saying *adios* to being mocked by Luke on a regular basis. But for some reason, the whole scene annoyed me. The way Nikki laughed extra hard at whatever Luke was saying, leaning in to touch his arm briefly. The way he looked at her like all he wanted was to kiss her. I'd always thought that once I had a boyfriend I wouldn't mind seeing how silly people got around someone they liked, but maybe I was wrong. Maybe I was just too **cynical** for my own good.

When Nikki finally tore herself away to come back to the car, the whole ride home was one long rant about how "intensely" she and Luke had "connected." I said I was glad to help out. And I was . . . right?

---

ogling: eyeing	**immaterial:** unimportant	**cynical:** negative
mortal: human	**extraneous:** unneeded	

October 31: Halloween

Just got back from the Halloween party at Megan's house, which means I come **wielding copious** amounts of gossip.

Megan, it should be noted, is one of the members of the **Triumvirate**. (They don't call themselves that—it's a **sobriquet** Nikki and I came up with freshman year to describe their ambition for absolute **dominion** over the social functions of our class.) Megan, Cecily, and Shannon are the three "coolest" girls in our class, as defined by . . . well, themselves. There's no need to describe them in depth, because they're as shallow as the kiddie pool. I think most high schools have some version of the Triumvirate. In summary, Megan's the **imperious** leader who has lots of money, and thus throws the best parties. Cecily's the pretty but **vacuous** idiot with the **unbridled** "Omigod!" enthusiasm. And Shannon, while clearly the smartest, is a witch whom I have **loathed** since freshman year, when I overheard her describe me as "insignificant."

So Nikki and I showed up late, partly due to her neurotic attention to the smallest **minutiae** of her appearance while getting ready. Such thrilling topics as the even distribution of self-tanner somehow became **fodder** for extensive debate. The sad thing was, I picked out our costumes—nurses, how original—because I figured it would be simple. But I forgot about Nikki's need to look absolutely perfect, for purposes of enticing Luke. Put that together with a nurse costume, and you have a recipe for getting-ready **longevity**.

By the time we got there, Luke was already the **epicenter** of a big crowd. He was dressed up as a monk—a monk who, **paradoxically**,

wielding: carrying	imperious: domineering	fodder: food
copious: plentiful	vacuous: empty-headed	longevity: long life
triumvirate: threesome	unbridled: unrestrained	epicenter: precise center
sobriquet: nickname	loathed: hated	paradoxically: in
dominion: power	minutiae: details	contradiction

was surrounded by girls. It was just too much. The sounds of you're-so-funny giggle fits **emanating** from his band of **cloying** disciples was enough to make even the most **stalwart** of stomach want to vomit.

"I'm going to get a drink," Nikki said.

And this from a girl who, like me, generally **repudiates** alcohol. We went down to the keg, at the end of the **gargantuan** deck behind Megan's **palatial** home.

High school parties—especially the ones that actually have alcohol—provide some of the best people-watching in the world. Megan's party was no exception. What looks like social **chaos** is, upon closer inspection, an organized group ritual. People gather in conservative clumps of the same friends they hang out with outside of parties. Everyone grasps their cups like security blankets. Some groups seem entirely dedicated to making themselves laugh. Guys **gape** at the girls they **covet**. Girls play **coy**, pretending not to notice, but are actually putting on a show with their radiant accidental smiles and **winsome** little hair flips.

Then the alcohol kicks in, for the kids who like to get drunk. A fair amount of guys start acting like **imbeciles**, **garnering** as much camera time as they can with un-funny jokes and **strident** cackling. The **pugnacious** drunks start fights. The weepy drunks cry.

Me, I tend to opt out of all the above in favor of the state of mind I know best—**sobriety**. Tonight I was the designated driver for Nikki and Jeremy, but the truth is I never really want to drink anyway. It just makes my stomach upset, and after seeing how stupid people around me act, why would I want to look like them?

First up was the Triumvirate **debacle**. On occasion, two members of the **clique** turn on each other, usually **spurred** by the passive-aggressive **conniving** of the third member. This time it was Cecily vs. Shannon, with Megan too absorbed in Luke to take part. It's hard to say what **trifle** caused the rift, but it somehow resulted in Cecily tossing her beer in Shannon's face. Shannon screamed

emanating: originating	**gape**: stare	**pugnacious**: aggressive
cloying: sickly sweet	**covet**: desire	**sobriety**: abstinence
stalwart: robust	**coy**: shy	**debacle**: disaster
repudiates: rejects	**winsome**: charming	**clique**: group
gargantuan: enormous	**imbeciles**: idiots	**spurred**: prompted
palatial: palace-like	**garnering**: gaining	**conniving**: scheming
chaos: disorder	**strident**: loud	**trifle**: little thing

indignantly that her shirt was ruined, then responded by dousing Cecily's shirt with beer.

The next vaudeville act was, for me, the most entertaining, and not just because it involved my best friend. Just past midnight, Megan cleared out her parents' **opulent** living room furniture and turned the room into a dance floor. By the time I made it inside to check on my fellow nurse, she was part of a group of girls all dancing around Luke like he was some kind of Greek god or something. I mean, please. He had to be getting a real rush from all that ridiculous attention.

I wasn't the only one who didn't enjoy the spectacle on the dance floor. My slouching, bleary-eyed boyfriend kept muttering angry comments from his spot on the couch next to me. "What is it about that guy?" Jeremy said, shaking his head. "He's such a tool."

I couldn't help half-wishing I were out there dancing too—not with Luke, of course. But Jeremy wasn't up for it, and I didn't want to leave him by himself.

After the big Luke-a-thon dance, as I correctly **surmised**, the rest of the night was **anticlimactic**. Before long, the party thinned out, and I could no longer **stifle** the yawns. "Let's go," I said.

"Gladly," Jeremy said.

I surveyed the dance floor for Nikki, to no **avail**. She'd vanished. Went back out onto the porch. No dice. Went back inside and asked the girls in the long queue for the bathroom if they'd seen Nikki. They all nodded **lethargically**, and one pointed up. I walked around to the front and went upstairs. A voice in my head was telling me that someone else was missing from downstairs, too, but I ignored the thought, focused on finding Nikki.

I heard them before I saw them. A familiar giggle, and little murmurings I couldn't quite make out. I told my legs to walk away, but for some reason I couldn't. I took two steps up, and . . .

I froze, my mouth falling open. They were standing in the

indignantly: angrily	**surmised:** guessed	**avail:** benefit
opulent: showy	**anticlimactic:** disappointing	**lethargically:** lazily
	stifle: cover	

hallway near the wall, their lips locked in a kiss like no kiss I'd ever seen before. Intense, like they were afraid to let go of each other, but still sweet and soft at the same time. They were so in sync I felt like they'd discussed it in advance.

Jeremy and I don't kiss like that. For some reason it was the first **coherent** thought I could muster. And I was sure it was the reason for the strange way my heart was squeezing.

I cleared my throat, "Um . . . excuse me?"

They broke apart and turned at the sound of my voice, but neither of them seemed too happy to see me. My face felt warm, and I couldn't meet Nikki's eye.

"I was about to leave. Just seeing if you wanted to come with," I said. I was going for casual, but apparently the weird high-pitched thing that happened instead wasn't under my control.

"Go ahead," Nikki said. "I think I'll stay right here."

"Right. Um, okay." I nodded, then headed back downstairs to find Jeremy, swallowing back the funny taste in my mouth.

coherent: rational

November 4: Chaos Never Dies Day

I was standing at my locker today, between third and fourth periods, minding my own business, when Jeremy stormed up—well, as much as he could storm on his almost healed ankle—and blindsided me with a stream of **invective**.

"I can't believe, after all we've been through, that you would do this to me. Pretend to be my faithful girlfriend, pretend that we tell each other everything because we're . . ." He made quote fingers. *"Best friends.* I can't believe I trusted you. I can't believe I thought you were different."

I was as **befuddled** as I was concerned. If not for the vein popping out of his forehead, I might even have assumed he was kidding. It sounded like some poorly written soap opera **tirade**. I glanced over Jeremy's shoulder. Were we on a hidden camera show?

"What are you talking about?" I asked.

"What am I talking about? Oh, I don't know. Maybe about the fact that my girlfriend has been meeting up with Luke Barton on the sly, at his own home!"

Oh no, I thought, wincing. Why hadn't it occurred to me that maybe he'd hear it from someone else and that it would look a whole lot worse than what it really was? I buried my face in my hands to cover up my deer-in-the-headlights expression.

"Great," Jeremy said. "That's great! So it's not even a lie then. I was really hoping you'd at least try to convince me. I can't believe this. Finding out about my girlfriend's **infidelities** from all of my teammates."

---

invective: criticism   **tirade:** outburst   **infidelities:** disloyalties
befuddled: confused

"It's not what you're thinking," I said. "There's nothing going on between us."

"How would I know that? How long have you two been hanging out?"

"First of all, we haven't been *hanging out*. He has tutored me, twice, and trust me, it couldn't have been more innocent."

"But why wouldn't you tell me if it was so harmless?"

Good point. Come on, Francesca. Dig your way out of this hole. I exhaled. "Okay. The deal is, Nikki was, and still is, totally head-over-heels infatuated with the guy. Remember how they hooked up at the Halloween party? But she had no context with him."

"Context?"

"Just stick with me. She had no way of getting to know him. So she came up with the **ingenious** idea of hiring him to give me vocab lessons to prepare me for my SATs, because he used to work for one of those SAT review classes or whatever."

"But you have a great vocabulary."

"I know."

"And why you?" he asked. "Why not her?"

"I don't know, all right! She didn't want to be too **flagrant** with her come-on or something. Girl reasons . . . you know . . ."

Jeremy shook his head. He didn't know.

I put my hand on his shoulder, hoping to turn the tide of his **dwindling** faith in me. "You saw Nikki at the party. You saw how **brash** she was in coming on to him."

"Yeah, which is why I don't get why she needed your help."

"But that's the thing—she didn't have the guts to do that until after she'd already laid the groundwork, seeing him each time she picked me up from the tutoring sessions." I had another idea to convince him. "Hey, who do you think is paying for lessons?"

"Better not be you."

"Of course it's not," I said. "It's Nikki."

---

ingenious: brilliant   **dwindling:** shrinking   **brash:** bold
flagrant: obvious

This **disclosure** seemed to calm Jeremy a little. The storm cloud lifted slightly.

"So Luke and Nikki hooked up, right?" he asked. "The night of the party?"

"Yes. Thanks to yours truly."

"So, technically, your job is over. You don't have to keep up the tutoring charade any longer."

I knitted my brow. For reasons I couldn't explain, the **prospect** of quitting the tutorials didn't appeal to me as much as it had until this moment. More specifically, the **concept** of *having* to quit the lessons because my boyfriend **mandated** it was kind of icky.

"I guess I don't *have* to," I said.

"But you want to?"

I **hedged**. "No, it's just that . . . I do think he's gonna help me get a higher SAT score, so maybe I'll get into one of those colleges where I'm right on the cusp, like maybe an Ivy League school."

"No!" He folded his arms in front of his chest. "I'm sorry, but I won't allow some surfboard-waxin' nimrod to take my spot on the team *and* my girl."

"But he's not taking your—"

"No more lessons with him. If you can't handle that, then that's it. We're done."

Witnessing this **insolent** command, I had to use all my stores of discipline to **quash** a surge of **antipathy** toward him. *What a baby.* But my mood **modulated** as I gauged the hurt look on his face. Was I being insensitive here? It really hadn't been fair of me to keep this from him, and he had enough reasons to resent Luke already. Besides, maybe it was sweet in some way that he was so jealous over me. Right?

"Okay," I said. "The next lesson will be my last."

"You *have* to have another lesson?"

"The next one's my last," I **reiterated**. "Promise."

---

disclosure: admission	**hedged:** dodged	**antipathy:** dislike
prospect: possibility	**insolent:** rude	**modulated:** moderated
concept: idea	**quash:** suppress	**reiterated:** repeated
mandated: commanded		

November 9: USMC Day

Been doing a lot of **pontificating** about politics these past few weeks. My parents always have CNN on in the mornings before we leave, and it's hard not to get sucked in to all the crazy stuff going on in the world.

However, my burning **zeal** for global affairs was actually *not* what inspired me, after a **laborious** twenty-seven hours of **deliberation**, to announce my **candidacy** today for Junior Class Vice President.

It was a last-minute thing. I had an **epiphany** of sorts, yesterday. I'll set the scene for you. It was a crisp, **serene** autumn morning. Outside the window, our lawn was strewn with **variegated** leaves, colorful, like a finger painting. The sounds of jazz Muzak—Mom's "easy listening" station—played in the background. It was an instrumental **rendition** of "Beat It," with a flute as a surrogate for Michael Jackson's voice.

I was sitting in our breakfast **nook**, leaning my stool against the wall, reading the Columbus High newspaper. There was a story about a student, Jimmy Thatcher, who got tossed out of CH in a **plagiarism** scandal. The guilty **verdict** against him had been—in the opinion of the student body (those whom I talked to, anyway)— flat-out **spurious**. But we were powerless to the **edicts** of The Powers That Be—in this case, Principal Adams and all his **cronies** on the school board. The article didn't name any names, of course, but it talked in vague terms about the unfairness of certain recent actions against a student whose guilt hadn't been proven to the students' satisfaction.

pontificating: preaching	**epiphany:** divine realization	**plagiarism:** copying
zeal: enthusiasm	**serene:** peaceful	**verdict:** judgment
laborious: difficult	**variegated:** multicolored	**spurious:** false
deliberation: consideration	**rendition:** version	**edicts:** laws
candidacy: standing for office	**nook:** alcove	**cronies:** buddies

That's when the epiphany came. *Student Disciplinary Committee*. We needed to create an elected board of students to balance The Powers That Be. If a group of kids that reflected the **disparate** opinions of the student body were allowed to attend the board members' **caucuses**, the students could take a stand for their fellow man in the **egalitarian** manner of this great country. Then maybe guys like Jimmy Thatcher wouldn't end up getting **bilked** by the system.

But how would I get such **progressive legislation** passed? I would run for Class President! Wait a second. Bad idea. I would lose. I wasn't that popular. Class Secretary? No, I hated taking notes. Vice President. Maybe. Yeah. Now, that was ambitious.

So I went and signed up today after third period. I've already started making posters. Jeremy totally supports my political **aspirations** and has been helping me with the posters. The **fundamental tenet** of my campaign will be, naturally, the establishment of the Student Disciplinary Committee. This is a big step for me. It's a **valiant** step toward becoming The New Francesca, which I **vowed** I'd do over the summer. I will hold on to my **convictions**. I'm gonna make it happen. I can already hear my **horde** of followers chanting: *SDC! SDC! Castarelli! Castarelli!*

---

disparate: not similar
caucuses: assemblies
egalitarian: democratic
bilked: tricked
progressive: favoring change

legislation: law
aspirations: ambitions
fundamental: basic
tenet: theory
valiant: brave

vowed: promised
convictions: beliefs
horde: crowd

November 17:
World Peace Day

Tonight was my last vocabulary tutorial with Luke. Aside from the Jeremy issue, Nikki was running low on funds and didn't have much of a reason to keep sponsoring my lessons now that she had the guy.

As soon as we sat down for work, I told him what the deal was, just to get all the pent-up **anxiety** out. It went just the way I'd rehearsed it. "I have something to say," I said.

"What's that?"

"Due to **extenuating** circumstances beyond my control, but more specifically due to my **expeditious** advancement under your **inimitable** tutelage, I have chosen to **forego** further **pedagogical** services."

"Excuse me?"

"This is my last lesson."

"Yeah, I know what you *meant*. But I don't get it." Luke scrunched up his face. He looked not only befuddled but a bit **rankled** as well. Annoyed. A part of me felt a little happy that he wasn't as psyched to cut off our tutoring as Nikki and Jeremy both were. Maybe I wasn't so superfluous, after all.

"I thought we had a deal so I could pretend I had a job," Luke said. "And get some extra cash."

Right. That was what Luke cared about, not hanging around me. God, how many times over could I make myself an idiot? "Well, deal's off," I said **brusquely**.

"Why? I mean, is it so **insufferable** for you to stop by my place for some weekly big-worded **banter**?"

---

anxiety: unease
extenuating: outside influences
expeditious: swift

inimitable: unique
forego: give up
pedagogical: instructive
rankled: irritated

brusquely: abruptly
insufferable: unbearable
banter: conversation

"Frankly, yes," I spit out. "And I really don't think I need the practice, anyway."

"Oh is that right?" Luke said. "Very interesting . . ."

I pressed my lips together and nodded **solemnly**. Luke began to inspect me more closely, almost like an **anthropologist** studying the behavior of a primate.

"What?" I asked.

"Nothing."

"Say it."

"This wouldn't have anything to do with Jeremy, would it?" Luke said.

"No. Not at all."

"Not at *all*?"

"Not really . . ."

"What's that mean?"

"Not *exclusively*, anyway."

"But was he a factor in the equation?"

"I don't know," I said. "Why are you grilling me?"

"Would you say Jeremy was an **integral** factor?"

"No. I mean, yeah sure, I mentioned to Jeremy that, considering how busy I've been, it seemed a bit wasteful to be spending time on these sessions with you. And he totally **concurred**."

"I'll bet he did. Looks like we know who wears the pants in your relationship."

Whoa. His **retort** was like a cruise missile to my solar plexus. Once I shook off the impact, I was **livid**. I stepped forward and pointed at Luke's chest. "I know you're not gonna pretend you know anything about *my* relationship with Jeremy and who does or does not wear the pants."

Luke backed up, hands raised. "All right, all right. Fair enough. All I'm saying is that it would be a shame if you miss getting into Yale or Stanford because you're being **submissive**."

---

solemnly: seriously
anthropologist: scientist of human development

integral: essential
concurred: agreed
retort: angry reply

livid: furious
submissive: obedient

"Oh, *really*. And you don't think it's a tad **presumptuous** of you to think that *you* would be the deciding factor in whether *I* get into Yale? You know, the ancient Greeks believed that humans were punished by the Gods for that kind of **hubris**."

"The ancient Greeks are dead," Luke said. "And you might be misunderestimating the benefit of fifty SAT points and an articulate essay in the admissions pro—"

"Did you just say *misunderestimate*? That's not a word."

"The president used it in a speech," Luke said. "So now it's kind of a word."

"And where did the president go to college?" I asked.

"Yale."

"There," I said. "I rest my case."

"You win. Way to go. High five." He put his hand up for me to slap.

"Why do you have to be such a wise guy all the time? Do you have a sincere bone in your body?"

"Of course."

"Oh yeah? Which one? Let me guess, it's one of those tiny little ear bones?" For some reason, I was suddenly outraged by his cool indifference to everything. I felt like going on the offensive. Luke needed to be kept in check. "You know, Luke. While we're on the subject of sincerity, I was wondering, what are your **intentions** with my friend Nikki?"

"My intentions?"

"Yeah. Like, are you planning on going out with her? What's the deal?"

"What is this? Are you on some sort of **reconnaissance** mission for her?" His eyes narrowed. "Is that what this whole thing is about, here?"

Uh-oh. Nikki would kill me if I gave her away. "Of course not," I said quickly. "But as long as I'm *here*, I figured I could ask."

---

presumptuous: assuming **intentions:** goals
hubris: arrogance **reconnaissance:** spying

"What do you want from me? I like Nikki. She's cool. Do I want to marry her? I mean, come on. I just moved here. One thing's for sure. I'm not going to throw my cards on the table just for your **edification**. If Nikki wants to know, she can ask."

"She doesn't have to. I've heard things. I know you probably don't care about Nikki. You just want to get as much as you can out of her. Then you'll move on to the next one."

"Whatever." He flipped his hand at me dismissively. "Thanks for the **prognostication** there, Adelphi."

"*Whatever*. That's the credo for your whole life isn't it? It's all good. Whatever."

"For the time being, yeah."

"Well guess what? You know, it's selfish, lazy people like you who inspired me to go into politics," I blurted out.

"Politics?" Luke asked.

"Yeah. I'm running for Vice President."

"VP, huh? Very impressive. But isn't that the kind of thing where the President gets to pick his own running mate?""

I glared at him. "*Junior Class* Vice President."

Luke **chortled**. "Oh man," he said.

"What's that supposed to mean?" Did Luke have to mock every single thing I ever said? Was it, like, his job or something?

He rolled his eyes. "Nothing. Forget it."

"Too late now. What's so crazy about me running for Vice President?"

"No, it's just like, even real politics is complete bull, and running for school government positions is even more absurd because there's no actual power. I mean, why do you want to be vice president? To really change things? Of course not. It's a popularity contest, to prove to yourself that people know you and think you're okay. Who gives a flying—"

"I do!" I yelled, a little louder than I'd planned. "I'm not running

---

edification: instruction   **prognostication:** prediction   **chortled:** laughed

to **substantiate** my popularity. It so happens that I have a political platform that I feel very strongly about. So don't give me this too-cool-for-student-government crap."

"All right," Luke said. "Okay, then. So tell me. What's your platform?"

"It's just . . ." Something akin to hyperventilation set in at the realization that whatever I said would sound super cheesy. "It's not like you actually care."

"No, seriously. Tell me."

"I think there should be a student disciplinary committee that has equal footing with the adults—"

"Wait a second, are you serious?"

"What?" I asked. "Why's that so stupid?"

"It's not. It's just **quixotic**. You actually think that, as vice president, you have enough political **clout** to do . . . anything?"

"Yes."

"Well, I hate to be the bearer of bad **tidings** here, but you don't. You'll be blowing up balloons for the school dance, at best."

"That's not true."

"But at least you'll know you're popular," he said **sardonically**.

I felt like I was about to explode. Why did I have to take one more second with this jerk, anyway? "Just forget it," I said. "You'd obviously rather sit here in your room and look down at everyone else in the entire world than actually take *anything* seriously. So you know what? This has nothing to do with Jeremy. I'm out of here, and it's one hundred percent my own decision. Okay?"

I was pretty proud of myself after that one . . . but the frustrating part was, on my way out, I turned around and saw that same stupid condescending smile plastered on his face, like he knew I couldn't stay away for long. Yeah, I'd show him.

---

substantiate: validate   **clout:** power   **sardonically:** sarcastically
quixotic: idealistic   **tidings:** news

November 23: National Cashew Day

Okay, fine. I miss him. But that's totally between us, okay? Not a single soul will ever know. And it's just because he's the only person who can actually keep up with my vocabulary, and I think it really was helping me prep for the SATs. That's all.

Anyway, Nikki **convened** an "**impromptu** emergency meeting" after school today, at Steak & Shake. I wasn't sure what it was about, but I had an **inkling** that it was about *him*, so I wasn't too pumped. We sat at our regular booth, the one nearest the jukebox. Rarely one for **circumlocution**, Nikki got directly to the point.

"I'm thinking about . . . *you know*. With him."

"You mean Luke?" I asked, almost **regurgitating** a mouthful of vanilla shake.

"Of course! Who did you think I meant?"

"No, I guess I knew. It's just kind of a shock."

"Well it shouldn't be. I've been talking your ear off for almost three weeks about how mind-blowing he is."

"Yeah, on the phone . . . you have . . ." I mumbled **incoherently**.

"What?"

"I said, you've been telling me on the phone, and by email. I haven't actually seen your face in almost a week."

"Oh, honey, I know. I'm sorry. But that's my whole point. He's just swooped in on my life and taken over my every thought. His presence . . . it's just so big and . . . overwhelming . . . and . . ."

"**Prodigious**?" I asked.

"Is that the word? I guess so. Anyway, so what do you think?

---

convened: called together
impromptu: last minute
inkling: suspicion

circumlocution: roundabout speech
regurgitating: spitting up

incoherently: inarticulately
prodigious: remarkable

Should I listen to my heart and just go for it?"

"Hmmm . . ." I slurped on my straw as a delaying **tactic**. My instincts were screaming *No way*, but I knew that wasn't totally **objective**, considering how **incensed** I was at Luke. Instead of blurting out what I really thought, I decided to do some careful testing first. "So, let's go over the pros and cons here. What are your reasons for thinking this is a good idea?"

Nikki snorted out a laugh. "I love it. You're so calculating about stuff like this. My reasons . . ." She slurped her straw and swallowed. "My reasons are that he's the most attractive, mysterious, interesting, **stimulating** guy I've ever met." She looked into the distance and smiled this big, dreamy, sickening smile. "He's the first guy I've hung out with who's smarter than me. Way smarter. Did I tell you he wants to be an anthropologist?"

"Several times," I said. "And you keep telling me how you love the fact that he's all independent and **enigmatic**. Which is great, but it reminds me of your scouting report on Jason Reynolds, who ultimately broke your heart because he was a total scumbag player. My point is, aren't you worried about Luke being a commitment-phobe?"

"No . . . I mean, we've been hanging out like three nights a week. I think it's pretty obvious that we're on the verge of going out."

"Have you discussed it?"

"Not **explicitly**."

"You haven't had the relationship talk? The where-is-this-going talk?"

"No, Fran. Chill out. I don't want to scare him off or—"

"Because I'm concerned that you're setting yourself up for heartbreak. I mean, I've never seen you so exposed like this, and I really don't trust this guy."

"Oh, come on. It's the twenty-first century. You don't have to have a ring on your finger to have sex."

"You say that, but I know for a fact that you'll feel seriously

---

tactic: method   **incensed:** angry   **enigmatic:** mysterious
objective: impartial   **stimulating:** exciting   **explicitly:** specifically

aggrieved if he disappears afterward and acts like you don't mean anything."

"Uh, excuse me," a voice said. Nikki and I looked up. It was the waiter, hovering there above us. He was new here. He had on the standard Steak & Shake uniform of goofy paper hat and a red bow tie. Steak & Shake bore some resemblance to one of those old diners from the fifties, with checkered floors and neon signs and oldies-but-goodies playing. Normally I **revered** this, but right now it just seemed **ersatz**. The waiter reached down to hand us menus.

"Actually, I don't think we need them," I said. "We know what we want."

"Okaaay." The waiter scrabbled for his pad and pen. "Go ahead . . ."

"I'll have the Frisco Melt Deluxe with cheese fries," I said.

"Got it." The waiter scribbled.

"And I'll have a bowl of chili and the house salad with ranch dressing," Nikki said.

"Okay, then." The waiter finished scribbling. "Thanks, guys."

As soon as he was out of earshot, Nikki leaned in and looked me in the eyes. "I think I know what's going on. Luke mentioned you two had an argument at your last tutoring lesson. Is that the problem here?"

"Not at all," I said. "I'm just worried that you're falling in *deep like* with him, like long-term-boyfriend, potential *love* like. And if that's the case, then this may not be the best **stratagem**."

"Why are you so convinced that he's gonna break my heart?" Nikki leaned her elbows into the table. In the background, someone was singing about a "Devil with a Blue Dress On." "Do you know something I don't know?"

"I just don't trust him. I think he's a player."

"Well, I guess we'll find out soon enough," Nikki said. "Because as soon as I get the chance, I'm going after him."

---

aggrieved: upset **ersatz:** false **stratagem:** scheme
revered: respected

It was before first period when I saw it—right next to one of my posters. My jaw almost dropped to the floor in **abject** horror. A huge picture of him, **smirking** and giving a snarky double thumbs-up. Beneath it:

LUKE BARTON FOR PRESIDENT OF VICE

Oh, no! He didn't! I looked around, clenching my teeth. There were witnesses. A girl from my pre-calculus class was staring at me. Beside the stairs, I spotted Eric Crowther and a few of his freak-a-zoid friends, looking up and down to cover up their ambulance-chasing curiosity to my reaction. Eric didn't look away though. He shook his head and bit his lip as if to say, *Whatcha gonna do about* that?

Instincts took hold, and I was suddenly speed-walking down the hall. I passed Eric and started running, **indifferent** to how **histrionic** it must have looked. I darted **mercurially** in and out of **aggregations** of people, negotiating hallway traffic.

Campaign headquarters was near the entrance to the gym. I caught it out of the corner of my eye as I ran by and put on the brakes like a cartoon character. I wiped my brow as I approached, trying to focus in on the man behind the booth.

Give me a break. Luke was wearing a cowboy hat, a leather biker's jacket, dark aviator glasses, and fingerless gloves. A boom box next to him was playing "Free Bird" at low volume. He was perched on a makeshift throne and held a staff in his right hand. A **multitude** of

abject: despairing, cringing	**indifferent:** uncaring	**aggregations:** crowds
smirking: grinning	**histrionic:** dramatic	**multitude:** huge number
	mercurially: unpredictably	

well-wishers **flanked** him on all sides, both male and female. The guys were **predominantly composed** of mulleted rednecks doing guitar solos, but with a few **inquisitive** pre–frat boy types in the mix as well. The girls appeared to be a **coalescence** of freshophomores **diverted** from gym class by the thick **miasma** of testosterone. Several signs were posted, with messages boasting varying degrees of **inanity**. The few that stick out in my mind are:

> DON'T BELIEVE THE HYPE
> VICE RULES THE WORLD
> FREE MONEY FOR ALL!

I charged right up to the front of the booth. "What is all this? Are you running against me?"

"I'm not running against anyone. I'm running independently, for the lesser-known but **imperative** office of President of Vice."

A few of his **underlings** cheered. Luke smiled.

"Oh, yeah?" I said. "What's your platform?"

"Platform . . . hmm. I guess you could say my goal is to perpetuate the ideals of vice and **immorality**."

"Cute. Are you mocking me?"

Luke shrugged. "Why do you get that idea?"

"Because if so, you've gone way too far. You've taken **uncouth** to phase two."

He smirked **suggestively**, then started counting to three. They were all looking at each other, reveling in the **camaraderie** of their shared political beliefs.

"Hell, no, we won't go! Hell, no, we won't go!" They pumped their fists in shared **gaiety**, chanting in unison, **flouncing** about like a family of splashing ducks. "Hell, no, we won't go! Hell, no, we won't go!" Even the girls in their gym shorts had joined in.

"What does that mean?" I **beseeched**. "Go *where*?"

---

flanked: surrounded
predominantly: mainly
composed: made up of
inquisitive: questioning
coalescence: grouping
diverted: sidetracked
miasma: haze

inanity: stupidity
imperative: essential
underlings: subordinates
immorality: corruption
uncouth: rude
suggestively: implying indecency

camaraderie: companionship
gaiety: cheerfulness
flouncing: prancing
beseeched: pleaded

Luke shrugged again. "That's unclear."

"Jerk." I turned and walked away. I found out at lunchtime that Luke got suspended for two days for his **grievous misconduct**. To that I can only respond, in the **immortal** words of Bart Simpson . . . *heh heh.*

---

grievous: serious   **misconduct:** bad behavior   **immortal:** undying

November 25: Thanksgiving

Ah, Thanksgiving at the Castarelli household. Per usual, Grandma Castarelli turned the Head Cook position into an appointed U.S. Army command post, barking orders at Mom and **censuring** me for my **lackadaisical** attitude toward the kitchen. Dad went downstairs to "work on his computer," aka evacuate the **premises**. Grandpa C went outside to rake leaves. My brother, Rico, was nowhere to be found. And this year's most significant cameo, Uncle Randy, was the exact opposite. He was **ubiquitous**.

I guess most families have some form of an Uncle Randy. He pulled up right before noon in his **dilapidated** RV, which was **yoked** to the back of a rusty pick-up truck. His horn sounded like a foghorn—*AAH-OOH-GA!* He dished out a few sloppy hugs and loud **salutations**, a cigarette dangling from his lips like it had a life of its own. "Looks like you're growin' into a woman," he said to me, a **dubious** compliment at best. He spent a **protracted** moment trying to convince dad that he had been **abstemious** for months, despite his blatant beer-breath to the contrary. When Rico and his little skateboarding friends **materialized** in the driveway, he tried to join in and ended up flat on his butt.

A half hour or so before the turkey hit the table, Uncle Randy finished off the last of the **potables** in his Winnebago. He made a beeline for our liquor cabinet, muttering his **rationalization** that he "only drank on special occasions." Experience has taught us that when he switches from beer to whiskey the results are **cataclysmic**, and this year was no exception. It started with an

censuring: criticizing	**yoked:** bound	**materialized:** appeared
lackadaisical: lazy	**salutations:** greetings	**potables:** drinks
premises: grounds	**dubious:** doubtful	**rationalization:** reason
ubiquitous: everywhere	**protracted:** extended	**cataclysmic:** disastrous
dilapidated: run down	**abstemious:** self-denying	

utterly inappropriate **anecdote** about an experience he had in Guadalajara. Say what you want about him, but Uncle Randy's a great **raconteur**. Still, the story got a little racy, and my grandparents weren't much amused.

Then came the momentous Dumping of the Mashed Potatoes. Luckily for him, they blended in well with the beige carpet in our living room. The climax came when Grandma called Uncle Randy a drunken **lout** under her breath. He **rebutted** by calling her a "senile fascist," and that was his death **knell**. Mom gave Dad "the look," and Dad asked Randy if he could talk to him outside. I heard Randy offering to **rescind** the comment, but it was too late. He spent the rest of the evening out in the Winnebago, listening to country music.

Thanksgiving went back to the family comfort-fest that it's supposed to be, so I retreated to my room, where I decided to write a letter to Luke, inspired by the crazy behavior of all my loony relatives.

> _Dear Luke,_
>
> _I just wanted to let you know that if your little campaign was directed at me, even **obliquely**, then it was rude and **indecorous**. You have already made your opinion about student politics known, so this extra smear campaign was flat-out **unwarranted**. The only reason I can imagine for you to mock something I take seriously in such a public and **defamatory** way is that you deliberately wanted to hurt my feelings._
>
> _What did I ever do to you? It is one thing to **flaunt** your **iconoclastic** views to the school to show how much cooler you are than the **peons** who campaign in hopes of making a difference. But it is another thing altogether to single me out for ridicule (the fact that both "Vice" and "President" are in your **fabricated** title cannot, after all, be a coincidence),_

anecdote: story	**rescind:** take back	**flaunt:** show off
raconteur: story teller	**obliquely:** indirectly	**iconoclastic:** radical
lout: thug	**indecorous:** impolite	**peons:** little folks
rebutted: argued back	**unwarranted:** unnecessary	**fabricated:** fictional
knell: chime	**defamatory:** destroying a reputation	

simply to amuse yourself. You think you're such a renegade, such a **nonconformist**. *I thought I was—***heretofore***—your friend. But needless to say, I am, hereafter and forevermore, not. Your friend, that is. But thanks for sharing your (rather* **paltry***) verbal knowledge, and good luck in the rest of your (completely worthless) life.*

> *Yours in infinite* **enmity***,*
> *I am,*
> *Francesca Castarelli*

nonconformist: rebel   **paltry:** limited   **enmity:** hostility
heretofore. until now

November 30: National Woodsmen's Day

I found out I won the election today. Principal Adams **divulged** the results over the PA system during last period. Some of the people in my health class clapped, causing me to **timorously** blush into my desk's wood **veneer**. When the bell rang, Jeremy was waiting for me, right outside the classroom's **threshold**. He held me up in the air like a pirate showing off his **looted plunder**, and after he put me down he **wrested** one of Luke's posters from the wall and shredded it. At first I was psyched at how supportive he was being, but then I realized that the **effusiveness** of his enthusiasm wasn't just about me.

"Babe," he said, his face practically glowing. "How cool is this? You just won the supreme popularity contest. Pretty nice having Jeremy Malone for a boyfriend, right?"

I felt like I'd been socked in the stomach, and it was even worse when he didn't understand why I was upset.

I know I still should have felt **cuphoric** about winning. A part of me wanted to do a victory dance on Luke's face. But for some reason, I also felt **chagrined** and a little guilty. Embarrassed at my own self-importance, and about taking my campaign and this whole SDC issue so seriously. Jeremy's words just confirmed everything Luke had teased me about. Had he been right, even a little? Had I really only won because I was Jeremy's girlfriend? Was the whole Junior Class Vice President role just one big joke?

---

divulged: revealed
timorously: bashfully
veneer: coating
threshold: entrance

looted: burgled
plunder: booty
wrested: tore

effusiveness: gushiness
euphoric: overjoyed
chagrined: ashamed

December 1: AIDS Awareness Day

I was sitting in the living room this evening after school, procrastinating on my English essay, wallowing in self-pity, and fending off waves of bad cramps. *Blind Date* was on TV. It's one of those dating shows you can't stop watching because it makes you feel better to know that at least you're not *those people*. This particular episode featured Gerald, a **turgid** Californian weightlifter with an orange fake bake. Gerald was big on first impressions. He started off by ridiculing his **robust** date's nutritional **shrewdness** because she liked pizza, then proceeded to mack on her with slimy come-on lines. "If you would **exude** a more loving vibe, I swear I'd rock your world," he crooned while trying to force-feed her organic pasta.

The doorbell rang. I got up, moaning. I saw in the peephole that it was Jeremy and creaked the door open.

"Come with me," he said. "I'm taking you somewhere, to celebrate your victory."

I smiled, feeling a little better. Maybe Jeremy's first reaction was the usual guy thing of making a big scene and taking all the credit himself, but at least he was coming through now. I turned off the TV and grabbed my purse. Out by the car, Jeremy insisted on blindfolding me, despite my protests.

"You said you love surprises," he argued.

He had me there. While tying the bandana around my eyes, he planted a soft kiss on my neck that melted me, the first **iota** of pleasure I'd felt in hours. We spun out of there in his Acura, me seeing nothing and him saying nothing, at least not that I could hear over

---

turgid: swollen	**shrewdness:** knowledge	**iota:** bit
robust: healthy	**exude:** give off	

the **dissonant** screech of some bad rock song. *He's being such a sweetie. Keep your mouth shut, Fran.* But as much as I wanted to respond to his romantic gestures with **sublime gratitude**, my body had other plans.

I know it's different for everyone, but the first day of my period is always the worst. It starts with the dull, persistent lower-backache. Then my stomach muscles are contracting in wave-like **paroxysms** of pain. There's dizzying nausea. Once, freshman year, I spent eight **harrowing** hours in the fetal position in my darkened room.

"I'm sorry to be annoying," I finally said, trying not to sound too whiny. "But could we listen to something a little more mellow?"

"Oh sure," he said. "I'm sorry."

He put on Sade's *Greatest Hits*, which has sort of become "our CD" after serving as background music to more than a few make-out sessions. And I must admit, the first few notes of her **luxuriant** voice **pacified** me somewhat. But mid-way into "No Ordinary Love," my annoyance had found a new focus.

"Um, about how close are we to our destination?" I asked, shifting uncomfortably.

"That's for me to know and you to find out."

"Because if it's any longer than ten minutes, I'm gonna wig out. I'm sorry, but it's just too sweaty and dark in here."

Jeremy **succumbed** and took off the blindfold, and rays of light immediately hit my eyes. I cringed and blinked a few times.

"Are you all right?" Jeremy asked.

"Yeah, I'm fine," I said. I had a bad feeling it came out kind of snappy, and he didn't respond, so I was probably right.

Finally my eyes adjusted to the light and I focused in on our surroundings. We were going north on I-65. To our far left, on the horizon, the sun was setting, a **transcendent** blend of periwinkle and **iridescent** salmon.

"Are we going up to Indy?" I asked.

---

dissonant: unmusical
sublime: splendid
gratitude: thankfulness

paroxysms: spasms
harrowing: distressing
luxuriant: lush

pacified: calmed
succumbed: surrendered
transcendent: awe-inspiring
iridescent: shimmering

"Maybe."

"Were you planning to leave the blindfold on for a full hour?"

"Maybe."

Which, as it turned out, meant "**affirmative**." **Fortuitously**, though, Jeremy's romantic skills are more finely **honed** than his kidnapping **aptitude**, because the place we ended up at was awesome. Located at the **pinnacle** of a skyscraper, the restaurant rotated slowly on its axis, clockwise, as we ate. The waiters wore suits with towels tossed over their forearms, and the cheapest entrée was like twenty-five bucks. Our table was by the window, so we got to see the full **panorama** of the city. I gushed thank-yous at Jeremy over and over, feeling like such a jerk. But he shrugged them all away, saying he wanted this night to be special. And it was. Even my period queasiness **abated**, that is until just a few bites into my filet mignon. I looked down at the swirling city lights below and felt myself chewing in slow mo, getting more nauseated with each chomp. The fork stopped on its way to my mouth. I clinked it against the plate and closed my eyes.

"Are you okay?" Jeremy asked. I felt his hand on my forearm.

"Please don't touch," I said. "I—I, um, I'm feeling a little sick. It's, you know, that time."

"Oh man." Jeremy's face flushed, and a flash of annoyance passed over his features. "Are we talking Vomitsville here?"

"No, I think I just need to stop eating."

"But you've only taken three bites."

"I know. I'm sorry. Please don't be mad at me for being such an **abysmal** date. Trust me, though, it's better than the alternative."

"I'll take your word," Jeremy said. He got all **taciturn** after that, but I understood why. I mean, he'd planned this amazing night for us, and my body had to go and ruin everything.

Still, I sensed something else was bothering him, which he soon **averred**. "You know, some people have been saying that it was his

---

affirmative: yes	aptitude: ability	abated: died down
fortuitously: luckily	pinnacle: top	abysmal: terrible
honed: sharpened	panorama: view	taciturn: silent
		averred: affirmed

way of flirting with you."

I frowned. "What? Whose way?" I asked, even though some-where inside, I knew.

Jeremy was looking down at his plate, chewing. "You know, with the whole President of Vice campaign. Some people are saying it's his immature way of flirting, but I think that's crazy. I think he's just being a **pretentious** jerk."

I felt my heart **lurch**. "Of course it is. I mean, *he* is." My thoughts raced, trying to piece together the **incongruous** logic of what he'd just said. "I mean, what could be flirtatious about that? It doesn't make any sense . . ."

"I can't say it's completely ridiculous. It's kind of like in grade school when you chase the cutest girl at recess. That whole deal."

I looked at him. He was doing that thing again, where he worked hard to pretend he didn't care. He still wouldn't look at me. Was Jeremy jealous?

"I hope you're not—"

"Forget it," Jeremy interrupted. "I knew you'd agree . . . How about a toast?" He lifted his glass of Coke. "To you, the new Vice President . . ."

I smiled and lifted my glass. "To . . . *me*," I said with a giggle.

"And to us," he added. "To taking our relationship to a higher **plateau**."

"Yeah," I agreed. "To us."

---

pretentious: pompous   **lurch:** pitch forward   **plateau:** level
incongruous: incompatible

December 10: Human Rights Day

When I got home tonight, my answering machine was blinking with three messages from Nikki, saying we had to talk . . . now. The urgency seemed to increase with each one, so I grabbed some special "medicine"—chocolate—from the emergency supply in my bedroom and took off right away to drive to her house. Mrs. Abrams answered the door, and even though I normally love hanging around to chat with Nikki's mom, this time I pretty much brushed her off with a quick hello. I ran up the staircase, taking in the pictures of Nikki and her sister, Claudia. The two of them get **incrementally** younger as you **ascend** the stairs, so that, at the top, they are just frizzy-haired little munchkins **gamboling** about naked in the sand-box. I did our secret knock and then opened her door.

"Oh, my God, Fran, I'm *so* glad you're here," Nikki burst out as soon as she saw me. She was lying diagonally across the bed, face down, not a good sign. Face down meant she'd been burying her face in the bedspread to cry.

"I brought you chocolate," I said, holding up the little yellow box. "Whitman's truffles."

She forced a weak smile, and I saw the telltale redness in her eyes. "Thanks," she said. "But I don't know if I can stomach anything right now. Could you just put it on my bed stand?"

Whoa. Not an **augur** of good things to come. The last time Nikki **snubbed** chocolate was after she'd been tripped by Gil Smith at a seventh-grade track meet. I reached down to hug her. "What is it? What happened?"

incrementally: increasingly	**gamboling:** skipping	**snubbed:** rejected
ascend: climb	**augur:** prediction	

Nikki slithered back on the bed and sat Indian-style, her back propped against the bed board. Pulling up a desk chair, I scrambled to get into listening position. "So, you know how I was planning to move things further with Luke, right?" she asked.

I bit my lip, a sense of dread coming over me. "Right," I said, eyeing her warily.

"Well, the last two times I've seen him we haven't had much alone time. But tonight, I was over there and no one else was home, so it was just us."

"Uh huh." The dread slowly spread through my body, reaching every limb until even my fingers tingled with **apprehension**. "So . . ."

"So we're in his room right, and we're listening to some funky music, and we're, you know, kissing and stuff. And we're both *really* into it. We're totally dissolved in the moment, in this perfect rhythm with each other . . ."

I swallowed, feeling the same bitter taste fill my mouth as the time I'd seen them kissing for the first time at the Halloween party.

"**Synchronicity**," I said, almost whispering.

"Exactly. It was amazing. The way he touched me just made me feel so . . . I don't know, so great."

I glanced away, trying to hide the swirl of emotions inside of me. *Focus,* I reminded myself. This was about Nikki. She needed me right now, and I had to forget about whatever I was feeling. I narrowed my eyes at her, still confused about where everything went wrong. "So then, did you guys . . . ?"

Nikki blinked a couple times, and I saw she was about to cry again. "I'm sorry Fran," she said. "I feel like such an idiot."

"Nikki, what happened? What did Luke do to you?" I jumped up and came onto the bed with her, putting my arms around her and pulling her into a hug. Now I was just getting scared.

"No, it's nothing like that," she said, her voice muffled into my

---

apprehension: nervousness   synchronicity: harmony

shoulder. She drew back and sniffled, then wiped her hand across her nose. "I had it all prepared, what I was going to say and everything, and I know this sounds ridiculous now, but I said, 'I want you, right now.'"

"Wow. You really said that?"

"Yeah."

"And what did he do?"

"He stopped . . ." Nikki tried to stay **impassive**, but her lower lip betrayed her with a faint quiver. She fought it off, squinching her mouth up tight. She's really **adroit** at not crying, way better than me. "He just stopped."

"What?"

"He went cold. When I asked what was wrong, he just said he didn't think we should."

I frowned, confused. Luke had rejected Nikki? A million thoughts crowded into my brain at once. Why would the ultimate player turn down sex with someone as gorgeous as my best friend? What was up with that? Beneath all of it, though, I felt such a huge burst of relief. For Nikki's sake, of course. Because I was still convinced it would have been a huge mistake for her to sleep with him.

"So, what did you say after that?" I asked gently.

"I didn't have to say anything." Nikki was shaking her head **dejectedly**. "I was just so pissed, and you know how bad I am at hiding my emotions. Here I am giving him the green light and he screeches the brakes. I was like, 'You jerk! You should feel privileged. How dare you!'"

I started to smile. "Wow, you really said that stuff to him?"

Nikki groaned. "No . . ." She ran her fingers through her hair. "I was in shock. I guess I was just hurt, you know? I couldn't process the fact that I'd been wanting him all this time, and he didn't want me back. I just wanted to get out of there . . . I didn't say anything."

The look on Nikki's face at that moment almost broke my heart.

---

impassive: emotionless   **adroit:** skillful   **dejectedly:** unhappily

It was enough to make me hate Luke Barton more than I ever had before. "And he didn't even try to stop you?" I asked. "He didn't say anything?"

"He said there was too big of an 'emotional **disequilibrium**' between us . . . that it wouldn't be fair to me."

Hmm. The thing was, as angry as I wanted to be at Luke, hearing that made me waver a little. It actually sounded like he was kind of trying to do the right thing. But this was clearly not the time to make that point to Nikki.

disequilibrium: inequality

December 14: National Bouillabaisse Day

In English class today, we discussed *Pride and Prejudice* by Jane Austen, which we just finished reading. Luke, who has been making **snide** comments about the book for weeks, started off by calling Austen an overrated "writer of Victorian soap operas." I led off in Austen's defense. I said it wasn't so easy to write a page-turner love story that was also a literary masterpiece—one chock-full of **incisive** social commentary that was still **pertinent** to today's social **milieu**. He agreed that it was obviously *supposed* to be a love story but **contended** it was a boring one at best and flat-out **refuted** that it contained even the slightest **modicum** of "social commentary."

To her credit, Ms. Cloisters said that oftentimes a critique says more about the reader than the writer. One other girl in class called Luke a misogynist. I **grandiloquently** argued that Ms. Austen wrote social **satires** in the same vein as modern movies like *Best in Show*, and that it was my understanding that Luke particularly enjoyed satire, so it seemed **ironic** that he didn't dig Austen.

"At least *Best in Show* is funny," was all Luke could manage.

Petulant little brat. What's funny to me is that Jeremy could be jealous of such a clown. And that Nikki could like him and want to share herself with him. I just wish he would go away.

---

snide: nasty	**contended:** argued	**satires:** spoofs
incisive: perceptive	**refuted:** denied	**ironic:** contrary to
pertinent: relevant	**modicum:** little bit	appearances
milieu: environment	**grandiloquently:** pompously	**petulant:** ill-tempered

December 17: National Maple Syrup Day

Luke emailed today to say he received my letter, which I finally decided to mail after what he did to Nikki. The **sniveling** twit said that it made him feel like dung. He also admitted that I was **deft** with words and that my verbal skills were worthy of **approbation**, but he claimed his tutorials were in part to thank for that. And since both of our futures were on the line here, he had a **proposition** for me. If I took a practice writing SAT test and scored less than seven hundred, then he would **resume** "word lessons" with me, **gratis**. If I got seven hundred or above, he would never bother me again.

I didn't hesitate. I deleted the message.

---

sniveling: whining   **approbation:** approval   **resume:** begin again
deft: skilled   **proposition:** offer   **gratis:** free

December 22: Forefather's Day

As part of a larger effort to support her in this time of need, I have spent the last twenty-four hours with Nikki. First off, Mrs. Abrams drove us up to the Fashion Mall north of Indy for some last-minute holiday shopping. Despite my mom's **unmitigated** adoration of bargains and window displays, I somehow failed to inherit the shopping gene altogether. Among my **peccadilloes** is that I could spend hours feeling fabric and staring at myself in dressing room mirrors, but if I'm not in the "buying mood," I won't even splurge for a Twix bar.

My **affliction** today was of a more seasonal nature: Whenever I go shopping for others, especially near Christmas, I only find stuff for me. Does everyone have this problem? I mean, who knew that jeans could be *this* flawlessly form-fitting, with a special "short" version for my **diminutive** legs? And when did they become so **exorbitantly** expensive?

Ultimately, with help from Nikki's mom, I finished all my shopping (and pretty much drained my checking account). In the **perpetually** impossible "male" category, I outdid myself. For Dad, I found a device that **discerns** when calls are from telemarketers and automatically hangs up on them. Dad's love of gadgets is directly **proportional** to his **animosity** toward telemarketers, so the gift couldn't have been more **felicitous**. I got my little bro Rico a Burton snowboarding jacket because he's Mr. X-treme Sports Guy. For Jeremy, I got a Puma watch with a wide leather armband that makes it look almost like a bracelet.

Dinner at Nikki's house is always a great time. Her parents are

---

unmitigated: absolute
peccadilloes: failings
affliction: burden

diminutive: tiny
exorbitantly: excessively
perpetually: continually
discerns: detects

proportional: relative
animosity: hatred
felicitous: fortunate

such **gourmands**. While she cooked, Mrs. Abrams told us the fairy tale about how she met Mr. Abrams—or Hugh, as she calls him—in Paris in 1963. As many times as we've heard it, it never seems to get old. When she got to the part where she chooses Mr. Abrams over the young, beautiful, African modern dancer/glassblower, I asked a question.

"But how'd you know you were picking the right one?"

"Well, when you're young," she said, "you can't. Your **criteria** is single-**faceted**, you know. You just want a cute guy, or a guy who can dance, or who buys you dinner. But once you've dated around some, you start looking for what I call The Whole Package."

"The whole package?" I asked.

"Yes. You have to find him attractive, of course. But there are also all the **intangibles** like intelligence and conversational skills and imagination and sensitivity and **beneficence** . . ."

"The Whole Package," I said.

"That's right," Mrs. Abrams said. "Don't forget it."

"Luke is The Whole Package," Nikki said **disconsolately**.

"No he's not," I said. "He's a powertool."

"Food's ready!" Mrs. Abrams said, in a stroke of **exemplary** timing.

Luckily, dinner was an **efficacious** way of taking Nikki's mind off of Luke. The first course was chilled pepper bisque with crabmeat and onions sprinkled on top. The entrée was pan-seared tuna with garlic confit and a side of ratatouille.

"Mmmm," I moaned. "This is so scrumptious. My parents probably had Domino's delivered tonight."

Nikki raised her glass of grape juice to propose a toast. "To my dorky parents, whom I love dearly."

"Aww . . ." We clinked glasses. Claudia stood up. "To me finally getting a cell phone." Laughter. More clinking.

Mrs. Abrams stood up. "Such a touching request, Claudia," she

---

gourmands: food lovers	**intangibles:** subtleties	**exemplary:** excellent
criteria: decisive factor	**beneficence:** good will	**efficacious:** effective
faceted: sided	**disconsolately:** miserably	

said, putting a hand over her heart. She raised her glass and gave Nikki a quick glance. "And here . . . here's to moving past failed relationships."

I looked at Nikki. Clearly not psyched. She looked like she wanted to say, "May I be excused?" We all clinked glasses anyway.

It was my turn. I didn't have anything planned. I raised my glass. "Uh, to Christmas Eve Eve Eve? Or maybe not. How about, to finding the one with The Whole Package. To falling in love and staying in love, like Mr. and Mrs. Abrams."

"Ohhh," Mrs. Abrams said. "How sweet."

We clinked our glasses and **imbibed**.

---

imbibed: drank

December 25: Christmas

I won't bore you with all the **odious** little details, because Christmas is always Christmas, especially the morning part. Jingle bells, jingle all the way. Ripping apart wrapping paper. "Oh, thanks so much!" Kiss and hug. More ripping. Frosty the Snowman. Rudolph the Red-Nosed Reindeer. "You're welcome! Do you really like it?"

As per usual, my parents demonstrated such **largesse** that I couldn't help but feel a little undeserving of all my gifts—including a digital camera and *another* pair of jeans. But at least Dad **lauded** the **utility** of the telemarketer zapper I got him. Rico seemed to dig his snowboarding jacket, but the quickness with which he put it back in its gift box seemed **duplicitous**. I pressed him until he said it was just that the colors were a tad **effeminate**. I tried to act like I wasn't hurt—no problem, I had the receipt—but it actually made me feel kind of **glum**. Mom seemed to love the coat and the book and the calendar, but it's hard to know for sure.

We spent most of the day lazing and tinkering about. In the evening, we **adhered** to the Castarelli family tradition of cruising around Columbus, looking at Christmas lights. It's the Christmas day event I look forward to most, one that **instills** a sense of joyful **consanguinity**. We drove through Mill Race Park, which sets up these **intricate** artistic light displays every year. My favorite design was the three random Christmas pigs dancing by the lake.

Then we drove through the neighborhoods, voting on our favorite houses. My dad and I both like the **gaudiest**, most **ornately adorned** houses with tons of colored lights, Santa and his reindeer

odious: horrible	**effeminate:** feminine	**intricate:** complex
largesse: generosity	**glum:** sad	**gaudiest:** flashiest
lauded: praised	**adhered:** stuck to	**ornately:** elaborately
utility: usefulness	**instills:** imparts	**adorned:** decorated
duplicitous: dishonest	**consanguinity:** kinship	

on the roof and plastic manger scenes in the yard. Mom prefers the more **elegant** displays with neatly ordered white lights, ribbons and wreaths. Rico remains **dispassionate**. But we all **chastise** the rich people in their McMansions for being too **conceited** to **deign** to put up any lights at all.

It's great to ride around with Mom, because she's a total gossip queen. When we drove past a familiar house (which boasted a pathetic **dearth** of Christmas lights), Mom said that that was where the Barton family lived. She **intimated** that Mr. Barton had already gotten a reputation around town for being a real mover and shaker.

"You know the Barton boy, right?" Mom asked me. "Didn't you study with him a few times?"

"Yeah," I said, wishing she'd drop the subject there.

"Wait, you didn't tell me that," Rico said. "I didn't know you hung out with Luke Barton!"

I frowned. "Why do you care?"

"Oh, nothing. Except he's, like, the seventh best skateboarder in the world," Rico gushed sarcastically. Right. I'd forgotten that Luke was internationally **renowned** in the sport my brother was obsessed with. "I heard that, on full moons, he used to vacuum out the water from suburban pools in Bakersfield and go skating with his friends," Rico went on.

"Sounds like a real keeper," Mom said.

Later on, we passed by Jeremy's house. Looking at his elegantly **illuminated** house, a rush of warmth overtook me. Jeremy wasn't too cool for student government, or Christmas lights, yet he was well-heeled enough to take me out to dinner at a five-star restaurant. I was lucky to have him. He was cute, and sweet, a somewhat **adept** conversationalist, and not unintelligent. He was about as close to The Whole Package as a girl like me could ask for.

---

elegant: refined
dispassionate: indifferent
chastise: criticize, rebuke

conceited: proud
deign: lower oneself
dearth: lack

intimated: hinted
renowned: well-known
illuminated: lighted
adept: skilled

December 31: New Year's Eve

Jeremy and I exchanged gifts today. He said he loved his watch, and I don't think he was faking it, because he put it on and didn't take it off. There's something about a watch that makes a guy more **tantalizing**. He got me a brown suede jacket, which is perfect because I never would have bought it for myself. And I'll definitely wear it sometimes, to like dress-up affairs.

As part of the ratification of the Perfect Girlfriend Act, pushed through the Senate of my mind on Christmas night, I gave him a back massage. It morphed into an intense hook-up session. Weird thing was, instead of reciprocating my masterful handiwork with the proper Francesca adoration, Jeremy became kind of distant afterward.

Fortunately, it didn't last too long, because we had a New Year's Eve party to go to. It was, of course, a Triumvirate party, at Shannon's house. Now, under **conventional** circumstances, I wouldn't go there for anything. But after much **prodding** from Jeremy and Nikki, both of whom **trumped** the party as a **veritable** "who's who of the junior class," I **begrudgingly assented**.

As expected, the party sucked. In Shannon's **overzealous** pursuit of **exclusivity**, the party felt a little thin, and it didn't help that it was in her basement. Nikki was all flirting with Whomever Wasn't Luke, with the hopes that Luke was watching. Jeremy was off playing Ping-Pong with his buddies. I was trapped in social purgatory on a chair in the corner, all by myself.

Finally, I got sick of it, and I propped myself up and walked toward

tantalizing: tempting	**trumped:** talked up	**assented:** agreed
conventional: normal	**veritable:** genuine	**overzealous:** overly eager
prodding: urging	**begrudgingly:** resentfully	**exclusivity:** selectiveness

the bar area. The tentative plan was to talk to the first person I saw. Unfortunately, that person, or should I say that *subhuman*, was none other than my **nemesis**: Shannon Teasdale, **prattling** mindlessly with two non-Triumvirates. I took a deep breath and made sure my face was smiling.

"This is a cool little bar area, Shannon," I said. "Great basement for a party."

"What are you trying to say?"

"I . . ." The blunt **churlishness** of her tone sent me into a mental tailspin. "I was just trying to give you a compliment."

"Because the only reason you get invited at all is because Jeremy wouldn't come without you . . ."

I took a half step back and tried to take in where she was going with this. Did I **provoke** her in some way? It didn't matter. There was a point where you had to step up. "That's funny, because the only reason *I* came here is because he begged me to come."

"Oh, really?" she said.

"Yup. Well, that and because I wanted to see what it's like to hang out with the *significant* people." I'd been waiting so long to say it. I wanted more. "But you know *what*, the thing I've **ascertained** here is, if this party . . ." I motioned behind me. "If you took this basement as a **proportionate** sample, then guess what? Looks to me like the significant people are a dying breed."

She looked confused. That was a start.

"What I'm saying is, not many people showed up for your big—"

"That's because I didn't invite many people," she cut in, "and apparently that was still one too many. You don't have to stay. The party wouldn't shut down without you. Considering all you've done is sit on the couch, and that you're dressed like a girl scout, I think we'd be better off without you."

I was wearing a plaid skirt and a white button-down blouse. "Actually, just so you know, I'm *supposed* to look like a girl scout. If

---

nemesis: enemy
prattling: blathering

churlishness: rudeness
provoke: incite

ascertained: determined
proportionate: balanced

you were up on what's in style anywhere outside of Columbus, you'd know that this is in right now."

"Where is *that* in?" Shannon scoffed. "Thailand? Malaysia?"

"Try New York, Milan, Paris . . ."

"Oh, right," Shannon said. "Let me guess. When you won the big election, your parents took you victory shopping in Paris, and you found that all the hottest boutiques were carrying the Catholic school girl look."

"What's the election got to do with what I'm wearing?" I asked.

"Oh nothing . . . I just think it's funny how you think you're all sweet, now that you're Vice President, when everyone knows that only losers run for school office."

I was about to go to town on her, when a body stepped in between us. It was Luke. I'd never seen him look angry before. "Only losers bother calling anyone else losers," he said **eloquently**.

"Exactly," I said, keeping my voice even despite my shock at having Luke Barton, of all people, coming to my defense. "And on that note, I think I'll go take a walk."

"Fine," she said. "Go."

I felt like I needed an **encore** here, a coup de grace. "But first I'm gonna fill up my little plastic cup." I flicked it with my finger, taking special care to **accentuate** the plinking sound. "Excuse me." I shouldered past her and went to grab a can of soda. It felt good. The New Francesca didn't back down from a fight. She met the enemy head on and emerged **triumphant**. Now it was time for my Victory Ginger Ale.

"If you're not staying," I felt a hand grab my wrist, "then you're not drinking my soda."

I turned and looked right into Shannon's smoldering eyes, fighting the urge to dump the ginger ale right over her head. But I knew better than to stoop to her level. "Fine," I said. I plopped the can back down on the bar, then turned to head upstairs. Jeremy shot

eloquently: expressively   **accentuate:** emphasize   **triumphant:** victorious
encore: repeat performance

me a quizzical glance from the Ping-Pong table but didn't come over. *Thanks for the support,* I thought. I charged upstairs, grabbed my coat and went outside. I was quite a ways down the block, and still **vituperating** Shannon with my thoughts, when I heard someone calling my name. *Too late now, Jeremy,* I thought, not breaking stride.

"Francesca, it's me, Luke. Hold up!"

I stopped, shivering even though it wasn't actually that cold.

"I brought you something," he said.

I turned around slowly, unsure what to expect. He jogged up to me, and I realized he was holding a can of ginger ale. He grinned when he reached me, passing me the soda.

I took it and held it for a second, staring at the can like I'd never seen one before. Then I popped the top and took a sip. "Thanks," I finally said. Luke was just standing there watching me, with that familiar cocky smile. I felt a strange urge to reach out and brush aside the blond curl that dangled over his forehead, but in a second the wind blew it out of his face.

"I wouldn't sweat that little argument back there," he said. "That party was lame."

"Yeah, seriously," I agreed. I paused, torn. "Listen, this is nice of you and all. I appreciate your sticking up for me. But you know, it doesn't change the other stuff you've done."

"Okay."

"Okay."

We stood there another minute, not saying anything. "So, can I have some?" he asked, gesturing at the ginger ale.

I frowned, then acquiesced, because after all—he'd chased me all the way down the street just to give it to me.

Luke sat down on the curb and downed some gulps of soda, then looked up at me. With a sigh, I sat down next to him and took the can back to finish it.

---

vituperating: berating

"So, do you know any of the constellations?" he asked, leaning back to look at the sky.

"Not really," I said. "Do you?"

"Yeah, but sometimes I like to make up my own."

I laughed. "Why doesn't that surprise me?" I teased. "Center of the universe much?"

He grinned, giving me a light punch on the arm. "Nice," he said. "But no, why don't you give it a try?"

"So, like . . . connect any random stars you can see into a shape, and give them a name?" I said.

"Exactly. Like, see that really bright one, right *there*?"

I squinted up at the stars where he was pointing, following his gaze. "Uh huh," I said.

"Okay, so, connect that to the one there, and there, and then that one, and what does that look like to you?"

I giggled. "A bunch of little bright dots?"

He groaned. "No, come on. Look closely."

I pressed my lips together. "Okay . . . um . . . wait, I know—it's like a skirt! And then above those, that's the top . . . it's like one of those stick figure girls on bathroom doors!"

Luke burst out laughing. "Not what I was thinking," he said. "But decent."

I settled back next to him, and we kept going, making different shapes and characters, and then telling stories to pull it all together. It was so much fun that when I heard the general uproar of horns and cheers that came with the stroke of midnight, I couldn't believe so much time had passed. I also knew I was in serious trouble.

January 1: New Year's Day

I hereby **pronounce** today Black Thursday. Jeremy isn't speaking to me. He can't believe I walked out on the party and didn't stick around to kiss him at midnight. I kind of think he could have come after me, but he doesn't see it like that. Then I called Nikki for support, but she was all miserable about Luke not finding her at midnight. Ever since their big moment that wasn't, she's been hoping that the "disequilibrium" between them would get straightened out, and he would realize he's madly in love with her. So when I admitted where Luke was, thinking she'd be psyched that he wasn't off kissing some other girl, she pretty much freaked on me. I kept apologizing and pleading my innocence, but the more I backpedaled, the guiltier I sounded. Yuck.

pronounce: declare

95

January 3:
Sleep Day

Gray Saturday. Things aren't getting much easier. Jeremy finally called. He grilled me about what happened outside with Luke, down to the last detail. For the most part, my story held up against the crossfire. It's not like anything happened between us. As for why I walked out of the party, when I filled him in on how obnoxious Shannon was to me, it seemed to **quell** Jeremy's rage for the time being, and the conversation ended with a relatively **gratifying** plea bargain—we "might not break up after all."

In other dreadful news, I asked my brother what he wanted for his birthday next week. He said he didn't want a gift, just for Luke to show up at his party. *No gift?* I had no idea Luke's presence held this much weight. After considering all the relevant factors, including my financial woes and my vow to steer clear of Luke, I told Rico it was a touching request, which, unfortunately, could not be arranged.

quell: soothe   **gratifying:** rewarding

January 4: Day of Transcendental Boredom

Due to a state of isolation-induced **monotony** bordering on **epidemic**, I actually sunk to an all-time **nadir** today. To cheer myself up, I willfully, even *gladly* submitted to an online practice SAT test. I got a 640 on the writing section, which is pretty **venerable** but still disappointing considering the **breadth** and **magnitude** of my vocabulary. The problem is, I've always sucked at standardized tests. I'm too slow. I'll sit for a full two minutes just thinking about what a word *really* means, and by the time my fifty minutes is up, I'll still have ten questions left.

I went to my bank's website to check my account balance—not an uplifting exercise. Christmas crushed me. As of now, I'm worth a grand total of $16.13, which, considering how I feel, is remarkably accurate.

Then I checked email. Two new messages. None from Jeremy. One junk mail, and this one, from Luke:

> *Dear Francesca,*
>
> *Our episode of* **tranquil cogitation** *together on New Year's has increased my desire to make permanent peace with you. So, if you are willing and able, I would like to extend my friendship, in hopes that, by way of some perfectly* **benign** *hang-out session, I could fully* **expiate** *my sins and leave*

---

monotony: dullness
epidemic: plague
nadir: rock bottom

venerable: respected
breadth: scope
magnitude: extent

tranquil: calm
cogitation: reflection
benign: harmless
expiate: make amends for

our ridiculous **imbroglio** *(which was, admittedly, my fault) behind us.*

> Sincerely,
> Lucas Barton

I thought about it. I came to a decision and, before my better instincts could **dissuade** me from **enacting** upon it, emailed him back.

Dear Lucas,

I appreciate your sincere apology, which, considering the **insidiousness** *of your offense, as well as its* **deleterious** *effect on my psyche, was a distinct step toward your* **exoneration***. The next and final step on your "road map" to* **amnesty** *is as follows: On the evening of January 13th, at 7:15 pm, you will arrive at my house at 3370 Wembley Lane, skateboard in tow, as a special guest appearance at the birthday party of my younger brother, Rico. You will doubtless be asked to do a few "Ollies," or tricks, or whatever it is you people do. You will* **comply** *with their demands in full and, if you perform to my satisfaction (I won't be present, per se, but will be observing from afar), then you will be fully* **exculpated***. At that time, we will see if circumstances permit a harmless hang-out session between us, as this appears to be an* **oxymoron***. Please post your reply within 24 hours, so I can relay it to Rico, who, for reasons I will never* **fathom***, has* **deified** *you as some sort of modern-day teenage Prometheus.*

> *Best,*
> *Francesca Castarelli*

---

imbroglio: mess
dissuade: discourage
enacting: acting

insidiousness: sinister nature
deleterious: harmful
exoneration: pardon
amnesty: forgiveness
comply: obey

exculpated: freed from blame
oxymoron: contradiction
fathom: understand
deified: made god-like

January 5: National Stonemason's Day

First day back at school. I wasted no time. When Jeremy got to his locker before homeroom, I was waiting there. I took no chances on the outfit—it was my colorful flower-print Quiksilver skirt and a tight black fuzzy sweater, the exact same outfit he'd complimented me on a few weeks earlier. My hands were behind my back. I wasn't smiling. The **prudently** chosen expression on my face was meant to **evince** sincere and thoughtful regret. The moment Jeremy registered my presence, the rhythm of his swagger faltered.

"I'm sorry," I said, pulling my hand from behind my back. A CD, three Toffifay candy bars (his favorite **confection**), and a card. It was a bribe. "It's for you."

Jeremy sheepishly accepted. "Great. Thanks. Excuse me . . ." He took a step past me and pretended to be working at his locker combination. "Who's Less Noobie-ens, anyway?" he muttered.

"Les Nubiens. They're French," I said. "You'll like it. It's funky but mellow, kind of like Sade."

"Oh."

I hoped he got what that meant.

"Listen, Jeremy, I'm really sorry," I said. "I mean it. But the thing is, you have to believe me when I say I was set up. Honestly. If you let this get to you, then Shannon wins. That's exactly the sort of **melodrama** she wants."

I could see Jeremy's jaw muscle working. Finally he turned and faced me directly. "Even if that's true, do you know how bad that looks for me, when you leave a crowded party and Luke runs after

---

prudently: wisely   confection: candy   melodrama: showy drama
evince: reveal

you like that? I mean, why'd you let him? Why didn't you just ask me to come with you?"

I frowned. *Because I'd thought he should just follow me, without having to be asked? But maybe I shouldn't have expected that.* "I know," I said. "I can only imagine what it looked like."

"Francesca, you have to promise me something. Promise me you'll stay away from him."

I thought about Rico's birthday party, about the email I just sent. "But—"

"No buts this time. Just say you're gonna do it, and then do it."

I let out a deep sigh. "Okay. I'll stay away from him." After all, I didn't have to hang around my brother's party. And steering clear of Luke was a good way to do damage control with the other hurting relationship in my life right now, too.

"All right, then," Jeremy said. "I'll take your word."

I nodded, wishing I didn't still feel all this distance between us. "Can I have a hug?" I asked.

Jeremy put his backpack on the checkered linoleum, **gingerly**. He wasn't quite looking into my eyes, but his lips had flattened out into something that **approximated** a smile. We wrapped our arms around each other, right there in the hallway, and I felt a little better.

---

gingerly: carefully   **approximated:** resembled

January 8: Go Get a Job Day

I went out and **procured** a job today, right after I used fourteen of my last sixteen bucks on gas. **Indigence** can be frightening, the way it constricts your freedom and makes you obsess about what you haven't got. You don't have to endure being a **pauper** very long before work starts to look appealing.

Instead of just driving around to restaurants asking for applications and looking for POSITIONS AVAILABLE signs, I figured it made more sense to just pick the **optimal** place to work and drive right over and tell it to them straight. The place I came up with was Viewpoint Books, my favorite place to be **frivolous** with my time and money. It's a small, locally owned bookstore located in the Commons Mall. The Commons is this *Star Trek*–looking cube of brown glass panels. It was designed by Cesar Pelli, some Italian guy who's famous for, as far as I know, designing freaky looking malls.

I walked right up to the counter at Viewpoint Books. The face above it was a familiar one—Agatha Renshaw, a girl from my school who's known for being a hippie type with strong opinions on stuff. I wasn't sure whether this was a good thing or a bad thing.

"Welcome to Viewpoint. Can I help you?" she asked in that hurried, **blasé** way that makes sales clerks sound like **automatons**.

"Hey, Agatha," I said.

"Hey," she said. "What do you need?"

"Well, I kind of need a job, and this is the only place I want to work."

"I don't know if we're hiring. But you can fill out an application."

---

procured: obtained
indigence: poverty
pauper: poor person

optimal: best
frivolous: trivial

blasé: unthinking
automatons: robots

"All right," I said. "May as well."

She gave me an application, and I sat down to fill it out. In the experience category, I put my two waiting jobs. In the special honors category, I wrote Soccer Captain and Junior Class Vice President. It was weird to see yourself defined as an **accruement** of accomplishments. While I was filling it out, Agatha went and talked to the owner of the store. He came and shook my hand. He said he didn't really need much help, but that he recognized me as a **recurrent** customer and liked that I said I only wanted to work there. So he hired me, right on the spot! Just for a few hours a week, but still—it seemed like it all came out perfectly. I took it as a sign that everything was getting back on track.

---

accruement: collection   **recurrent:** repeat

January 13: Rico's Birthday

All of Rico's chirping, shoulder-punching, baggie-clothed, hair-gelled friends showed up over an hour early for his party. I know this wasn't out of **fealty** toward Rico, but just because of the Luke cameo. This freaked out my mom, who **naïvely** expects her life to stay within the **strictures** of her daily planner. I solved her dilemma by breaking out that Old Faithful of male distractions: PlayStation.

This **satiated** them for a good forty-five minutes. I stood there, listening to them chatter. They're at that age where girls are starting to become the thing, which means **bravado** is of utmost importance.

By the time they started getting **restive**, Mom was ready to begin the party. Rico had told her repeatedly that the key to the party was **brevity**. The only elements he **sanctioned** were an ice cream cake (nothing written on it), gift unwrapping, and music (all songs pre-approved). It was the first time I'd ever been to a party where the birthday person was able to successfully **proscribe** the singing of "Happy Birthday."

Toward the completion of the gift unwrapping, the boys were already **rhapsodizing** about Luke. He was five minutes late, then ten, then twenty. I went from being irritated to internally **haranguing** him for his **negligence**. *You promised. You owe me. These kids look up to you.* At around 7:40, Rico walked up to me, and his **hapless** expression was enough to break your heart in half. "What's going on? You weren't kidding when you said he would show . . . right?"

"No . . . no . . . be patient," I said. That's when the **foreboding** sense of dread kicked in. Would he not come? If this was a hoax, if

fealty: loyalty	**bravado:** boldness	**rhapsodizing:** praising
naïvely: innocently	**restive:** restless	**haranguing:** criticizing
strictures: limits	**brevity:** briefness	**negligence:** inattention
satiated: satisfied	**sanctioned:** allowed	**hapless:** miserable
	proscribe: ban	**foreboding:** ominous

he was so **callous** that he would set me up for this big of a fall, then this was *it*—his final, most unforgivable **transgression**. I heard a scratching sound that made my ears perk up like a rabbit's at the snap of a twig. "Hey, wait a second," I said. But my brother and his pubescent munchkin buddies were a step ahead of me, clustered against the living room window.

"Dude!" one of them yelled. "That's so hardcore!"

The whole **raucous** throng of thirteen-year-olds scrambled outside, laughing and crying, "He's amazing!" His arrival couldn't have been timelier. I knew Luke planned it that way, for the same reason the Rolling Stones never show up at the time printed on the ticket stub. *Own the crowd.* I bounded the stairs three at a time and set up shop beneath my bedroom window.

He had a whole course set up. It was **circumscribed** by the grass on two sides, the garage on the other, and Luke's rusted-out pickup truck parked at the end of the driveway. Inside was a **labyrinthine** skating course with a ramp thingy, pylons, and this triangular-shaped metal bar like a staircase **balustrade**. He was wearing earphones, tuned out to things worldly, flipping up and back on the ramp, **delineating** the shape of a "U."

I was more impressed by his **temerity**. Skateboarding, the way he did it, looked like a surefire **excursion** to the hospital. But it was like walking to him. Luke kept his headphones on and carved out figure eights. I reached down and—my face concealed by my half-drawn Venetian blinds—opened my window. A gale of cold air swept across my face. Luke jumped onto the opened tailgate and started wiggling around on the bed of the truck. But the crunch of his wheels was soon drowned out by the roar from his **rollicking legion** of fans. Luke flipped his board up into his hand, and with the other hand, pulled his earphones from his ears.

Luke lifted off. My mouth **involuntarily** opened into an "O" shape.

---

callous: unfeeling
transgression: misbehavior
raucous: wild
circumscribed: confined

labyrinthine: maze-like
balustrade: railing
delineating: defining
temerity: boldness

excursion: outing
rollicking: high-spirited
legion: crowd
involuntarily: automatically

"And then you've got your grind tricks. Grinding's fun because you get the sense of gliding through the air in slo mo, like this . . ."

"All right, now, Rico gets to do the first trick!"

Rico slapped his board onto the ground and got a running start. He glided on it for a few feet, pushing once, and then did some sort of strained jumpy thing. "Yeah!" Luke yelled. "Nice move! Now everybody else join in!"

They all cascaded onto the driveway and started **cavorting** around on their skateboards, like a swarm of contented bees. Luke unleashed a big smile in the general direction of the house. I pulled away from the window. What could I do? You had to give props where props were due. That was quite a **coup** he'd pulled off.

---

cavorting: frolicking   **coup:** brilliant act

January 26: Day of Absolution

Today I got an email from Luke.

Dear Francesca,

*I believe I have complied with my end of our **arbitration** (in spades), without so much as a thank you from you. But so be it. I will assume that I'm **absolved** of all guilt. Let's fast forward to the matter of our hang-out session. Perhaps it would work better for you if I **exhumed** some tangible motive for us to hang out. Which **segues** nicely into the following question: Did you ever get around to taking a practice exam? Because one of the things I'd been meaning to tell you was, the SAT is less about how much vocabulary (or math) you know. It's a game, and you have to play the right way.*

*See, America thinks it's meritocratic—that people gain access to schools and cultural capital because of intelligence and hard work. But the truth is, rich kids from big cities and the suburbs are taking courses for $800 that prepare them for the SAT, while **penurious** kids from the South Bronx don't have that option. But I **digress**. The point is, since you have the option of getting an advantage for free, you may as well take it. I can show you things that will improve your score. That provides, in my opinion, **sufficient** motive for you to rationalize hanging out with me. Do you agree?*

Luke

---

arbitration: negotiation
absolved: forgiven
exhumed: dug up

segues: leads
penurious: needy

digress: wander
sufficient: enough

February 2: Groundhog Day

Punxsutawney Phil must have seen his shadow today. I think things are looking up for me. I wrote an editorial in the school paper that the editor-in-chief called "brave." I got compliments for it today at school.

Open Letter to Principal Adams

Dear Dr. Adams,

In my recent campaign for Junior Class Vice President, I pledged that I would create a Student Disciplinary Committee. It only makes sense that the perspective of students should be considered in disciplinary matters with potentially grave consequences, such as expulsion. If you would **abrogate** *or at least* **amend** *the* **antiquated** *policies now in existence and permit a group of students to offer their perspective, I'm convinced that it would stem the tide of student-wide discontent that has occurred after past controversial disciplinary measures. Confidence in your leadership, Dr. Adams, as well as in the forces of The Powers That Be, would be totally solidified.*

Sincerely,
Francesca R. Castarelli

abrogate: end   amend: change   antiquated: old

111

Not bad, right? So anyway, Dr. Adams called me down to his office during fifth period. The meeting was pretty **cursory**, which was good because I was sweating bullets. I had to wipe my clammy hands on my pants before shaking his hand. Dr. Adams was cool as a cucumber. He said that he admired my **initiative**, and that he would take my idea up with the members of the board. Meanwhile, I should draw up a proposal delineating the specifics of my plan, including how many students would be on the committee, and how they would be nominated.

Riding a wave of optimism, I walked right up to Luke after English class. The more I'd thought about it, the more I felt like it was no big deal to just get a little more SAT prep help from him. I knew I'd have to be careful not to let Jeremy find out since he was so crazy about the whole thing, but wasn't it worth it if it meant the difference for me getting into a good college? Not that I'd ever admit to Luke that I think that's the case or anything.

So, anyway, first I thanked Luke for his heroic performance at Rico's birthday party. Then I said I wanted to start tutoring with him again, and we decided to schedule a time for next week.

cursory: brief   **initiative:** proposal

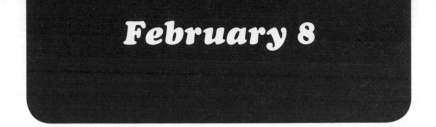

I definitely did the right thing. It's like Luke is this totally different person lately. He asked me today if we could have our lesson Wednesday night, but I told him Thursday night worked best for me. He said he'd made other plans for Thursday, but he could probably **defer** them or move them up. I said that would be very **conciliatory** of him and then went to my last-period class feeling good.

defer: postpone   **conciliatory:** appeasing

February 8 (Later)

Nikki showed up at Viewpoint Books tonight, in the middle of my first shift. I was glad to see her, because after a week of debating, I knew I had to tell her about the lesson I was having with Luke. Especially now that we had a real date and everything. I mean, not a *date* date—you know what I mean!

Keeping a secret from your BF is one thing, but you just don't do that to your BFF. I just hoped I could make her understand that this had nothing to do with what had gone down between them. I mean, she was the one who had the idea in the first place that I could use some help with my SAT score, right?

But it turned out I didn't even have to worry. Because before I could say anything, she came out with her big news—Luke had asked her out on a "real date," with dinner and everything.

"Wow. I don't know what to say." I really didn't. It was a total turnaround.

"Say you're happy for me!" she said, her silly, goofy grin getting even sillier and goofier. "Fran, this is exactly what we wanted!"

We? Somehow I was having trouble mustering a silly, goofy grin of my own.

But it was okay, because she didn't seem to care about my reaction. She was too busy raving about how this was her watershed moment and she needed my advice. I kept shushing her and **admonishing** her to pretend she was a customer, but she was too **elated** to calm down. Finally, I convinced the manager to let me take my break then because my friend had a personal emergency.

---

admonishing: cautioning   **elated:** overjoyed

"So, what night are you going out?" I asked as we walked toward the food court.

"Well, he originally said Thursday at lunch, but then something came up later so he called to ask if we could go on Wednes—"

"You mean, *this* Thursday?" I asked.

"No, I said we changed it until Wednesday."

"But you originally had it planned for this Thursday?"

"Uh, yeaa-uuh. Fran, that is so *not* the **crux** of the story. Sometimes it amazes me that you can be so smart and yet so clueless. Anyway . . ."

Nikki continued on a mile a minute, but my brain was stuck like a CD skipping. *He said his Thursday night plans could be changed. So he rescheduled their date around . . . us?* Why would he have done that? Didn't a first official date with Nikki rate higher than a stupid vocabulary lesson with me?

". . . So what do you think, Fran? Should I do it?" she asked.

"Huh?" I asked, snapped from my **reverie**. "I'm sorry. What?"

"Okay, I'm going to say it slowly for you. Should . . . I . . . ask . . . Luke . . . to . . . the . . . Valentine's . . . Day . . . Dance?"

"Oh," I said. "*That.* I don't know. I don't think so."

"Why not? You were supposed to say yes."

"I think you know why," I said. "Who was it again that told me that relationships are like a teeter-totter, and since guys are **inherently** heavier, girls need to do whatever it takes to maintain the balance and weigh down their side?"

"Did I say that?" Nikki scrunched up her face, **confounded**. "If so, I was just talking trash, because that **analogy** doesn't even make sense. As a woman, you want to be the one in the air, up on a pedestal."

I picked a straw wrapper off the table and crumpled it with my fingers. "Exactly. You want to be the **exalted** one, which is why you should *not* ask him and not mention the dance at all. Let him pursue you."

crux: core
reverie: musing

inherently: essentially
confounded: confused

analogy: comparison
exalted: glorious

"Yeah, that *sounds* great. But then who do I go to the dance with?"

"Who knows? Maybe Luke's already planning to invite you."

"But what if he's not?"

"Who cares?" I **posited**. "At worst, you miss the stupid Valentine's Day Dance. At best, you go with someone else. I'll bet you've already turned some poor guy down anyway."

"No . . . I mean, just one."

"Who?"

"Brant Durgin."

"What? But he's so cute! You used to always flirt with him."

"Yeah, but that was when he was going out with Vanessa. I just wanted to see if I could tempt him."

"You're awful." I smiled and leaned against the booth. My fingers were ripping the straw wrapper into shreds. "Listen, the thing is, it's a game. You're the one who taught me that, Nikki. Sometimes it helps to show a guy you don't need him."

Nikki cocked her head to the side, staring at me like she was only just now seeing me there across from her. "You know, sometimes I feel like you only give me one type of advice with Luke. I don't know whether to listen, because you're always telling me to hold back. Is there something more—something you're not saying?"

"What are you talking about?" I said, my heart skipping a beat. "What, like I have some kind of **ulterior** motive?" I met her gaze, then looked away, feeling suddenly awkward.

"You said it, not me," Nikki said. "All I know is that you never seem like you really want us to get together. Even now, when he's doing everything right."

"That's crazy," I said, forcing out a laugh. "I have a boyfriend, and you're my best friend. You asked my advice, and I gave it." I shook my head at her for a second, letting it sink in. "You know what? Do whatever you want." I glanced down at a watch that wasn't there. "I have to get back to work."

---

posited: put forward   **ulterior:** hidden

February 10: Opposite Day (aka, Antithesis Day)

So I don't know why I made the decision right then, while Jeremy and I were kissing in our usual spot in his basement, wedged in between square-shaped sofa stools, listening to Les Nubians. But suddenly it hit me that I'd be repeating history if I kept the tutoring thing from Jeremy again. This time, I had to tell him the truth and find a way to make him understand.

The next time we took a break for air, I pulled back and cleared my throat. "Listen, Jeremy, there's something I have to tell you," I said. Great—why'd I have to phrase it like that? Way to make it sound much worse than it was.

Jeremy's brow furrowed. "What's up?"

I took a deep breath. "The thing is," I began, "I had a long talk with my mom last night about college and stuff, and we've decided I should start up more tutorials with Luke . . ."

Jeremy pulled away from me, all ruffled. *Flustrated.* It's a word my soccer coach used all season long—one that, **incidentally**, doesn't exist. But the word captured his response perfectly. He cocked his fist back and punched the sofa pillow.

"Easy, killer," I said.

"You and your mom came to this decision together?" he asked, **incredulous**. "Women are so crazy."

I knew Jeremy. He could hold his ground. I was going to have to hold mine—even if it wasn't absolutely, exactly, the whole truth. "Listen, Jeremy. I'm gonna do it whether you agree with it or not. And you watch, I'll get a seven forty on my SAT, and then I'll get

---

antithesis: exact opposite   **incidentally:** by the way   **incredulous:** disbelieving

into Harvard and Stanford, all the Ivys."

"Big deal. Save your parents the hundred grand and get a full ride to IU. It's a great school."

"I love IU," I said. "It's just that . . . whatever, maybe I'm just a superficial glory-hound. I'm competitive. Deal with it. Anyway, that's why I'm gonna continue to work on my vocabulary . . . with Luke."

Jeremy hunched his shoulders and didn't speak. He was pleading the fifth, which meant he wasn't going to take a stand. I put a hand on his shoulder and backed myself onto his lap. I craned my lips to the right and kissed the side of his mouth. "Don't worry. You're the only guy I want," I said, hoping a good dose of cheeseball sentiment would do the trick.

February 11: Day Before Lincoln's Birthday

Nikki just called and woke me up. I was in that deeply relaxed state of half-sleep that comes right after you set your book down but before you're fully conked out. I looked at the clock—12:47.

Nikki was pretty **delirious** herself—but in a more energetic way. She was rushing her fragmented thoughts and giving me the events all out of order. The conclusion, which came first, went something like this: "I'm sick of it. This is it. I've had enough. I'm through."

"Through with *what*?" I responded, blinking awake.

"With him. He's such an egomaniac. He thinks he's so much better than everyone else . . . This whole time, I thought things were getting better, and I had no clue. I feel like such an idiot! Fran, I'm so sorry for not trusting you. You were totally right about him."

"Nikki. Stop. Rewind. Explain."

"I asked Luke to the dance. At first he kinda laughed and said he'd never been to a dance in his life. So I said, yeah, they were stupid and we didn't have to go. We could just hang out that night. That's when he said that he was having a *visitor*. And I was like, *a girlfriend*? And he was like, *not exactly*. And I was like, what does not exactly mean? And he said that they had been going out when he left California, so even though they broke up he wasn't sure what it would be like when she comes to see him . . ."

I swallowed, trying to process this latest piece of information. Luke had a girlfriend back home? One he still had ties to? So what was he doing asking Nikki out on a date? Hadn't he already put her through enough? I felt a sudden surge of appreciation for Jeremy.

delirious: feverish

121

Sweet, dependable Jeremy. There I was getting annoyed all the time at how jealous he got over me. That was a lot better than being a player like Luke!

"Oh, Nikki," I said. "I'm so sorry."

"Can you believe it?"

"What a dog," I said.

"I know, *I know*! And he even told me her name."

I cringed. "Do I want to know?"

"Brittany."

"Oh, my God. Like Spears? Like Murphy?"

"Exactly."

"So wait—is he taking her to the dance?"

"That's what I asked. And he said he hadn't planned to, that it was up to her. She only has a few days in town, so everything's up to her. I asked him what he was doing asking me out when he had this ex-girlfriend coming to town, and he said I'd read it all wrong—that our date was just supposed to be a friends thing or something stupid like that. He said it had been a while, and he thought we could "chill" together now without any weirdness."

"Nikki, I'm so sorry," I said again. "What're you gonna do?"

"I don't know. You know, I don't even want to talk about it anymore. I'm sick of the whole thing. I'm sorry I woke you up."

"Don't worry about it, Nik. I'm totally gonna rail on him tomorrow at our . . ." I caught myself and stopped. I'd never ended up telling her about the tutoring lesson, because how could I after she said he'd moved their date because of it? I'd hoped that by the time I actually went, everything would be fine because they would have had their date, and she wouldn't have cared anyway. But now was the worst time possible to give her one more reason to cry herself to sleep. "After class, at school," I finished lamely.

"Thanks Fran, that's sweet of you. But it'd probably be better if you didn't. I don't want him to know he got to me. I'm gonna go now. You go back to sleep. Sorry I woke you up. Bye, Frannie."

"Bye," I said.

I hung up, then lay back in bed, staring at the ceiling. Great. Now I was wide awake and more confused about everything than ever.

February 12: Abraham Lincoln's Birthday

I was late to the tutorial, but Luke hadn't even been in school that day so I wasn't sure what was going on anyway. During the whole ride over to his house I rehearsed my **diatribe**. He was either being insensitive or just clueless, and regardless, it was toying with Nikki's heart, and that was inexcusable. She was my friend, and I had every intention of protecting her. So, if he really liked her, he'd better start being a gentleman. And if he didn't, he'd better leave her alone. This was what I was thinking as I stood on Luke's porch, waiting for someone to answer the door.

But the second I saw Luke's face, my entire plan **dissipated**. In my rehearsals, I had been picturing him the way he'd always been—self-possessed, with that **supercilious** air of looking down at you. But his blue eyes were a shade of gray, and rimmed with red, and his shoulders slumped down at his sides.

He blinked when he saw me. "Hey, Francesca," he said, looking confused. Then something seemed to click in place. "Oh, right, tutoring. Sorry, I totally forgot." He ran his hand through his curls, sagging against the door frame. I recognized the hopelessness in his voice. It was the same **inconsolable** tone that used to bug me when Snuffleupagus used it on Sesame Street. But it was so out of place coming from Luke.

"What's wrong?" I asked.

He stared **wistfully** in the general **vicinity** of the ground behind me. "Come on in." He turned and walked down a dimly lit hallway. I followed Luke through the kitchen. There was the sound of scurrying

---

diatribe: attack
dissipated: dissolved

supercilious: arrogant
inconsolable: heart-broken

wistfully: sadly
vicinity: direction

footsteps and the squeak of a door closing. We went past a room I'd never seen before—an aqua blue office space with African masks and a fish tank filled with **aquatic** life.

We ambled up a flight of stairs and into Luke's bedroom. Jazz music was playing—the **dolorous** bleats of a tenor saxophone. Luke shut the door.

"What's going on?" I asked. "Is everything okay?"

Luke looked at me. "My Aunt Denise just died."

"Oh, my God," I said. "I don't—Luke, I'm so sorry."

He nodded, then sank down into his desk chair. There was a framed photo on his desk, of a woman with red hair cuddling her cat and smiling at the camera.

"Is that . . . ?" I trailed off, and Luke gave another brief nod.

"She loved that cat," he said. "She always loved her cats. She had, like, fifteen or something. I mean, not all at once."

He smiled, a small smile, and I smiled back.

"We knew it was coming for a while," he continued. "But it still felt like a shock, you know?"

"I'm so sorry . . ." A wave of **compassion** swelled within me, causing my eyes to tear up.

"Please don't do that," Luke said. "Maybe we should go outside."

We went for a walk. For a while we didn't say much. We crossed over National Road, the dewy grass **saturating** my shoes, and then ducked under a row of trees to the Oil Can Church. That's what we've always called it, because it looks like this big ol' **colossal** oil can. It has one **immense** spire that cuts way up into the sky, which is pretty stunning if you sit there and look at it.

"North Christian Church," Luke said, breaking the relative silence of whizzing cars and chirping crickets. "I don't go to church or anything. But this is where I spent a lot of time, late at night, when I first got here."

"Why?"

---

aquatic: sea	**compassion:** sympathy	**colossal:** huge
dolorous: mournful	**saturating:** soaking	**immense:** huge

"Depressed. You know, missing friends. Feeling sorry for myself."

"Right." I pointed up. "So d'you know that cross up there is six feet tall?"

We leaned way back and craned our necks. At the top of the church's spire was the jet-black **adumbration** of a cross that looked roughly the size of a small bird.

"I didn't know that," Luke said. "But I did know it's designed by the dude who did the St. Louis Arch."

"Really? I thought it was his son. Saarinen."

"Whatever. One of those guys . . . Hey, wanna go check out the playground?"

"Sure."

We headed over and started out on the swings for a while, then climbed across the swinging bridge that linked the slide with the monkey bars. There wasn't much to do on the bridge but bounce up and down and laugh about it. Luke stomped past me and **artfully** pulled his way across the monkey bars. I ran down the slide at break-neck speed, then ran back up and did it again. Luke hopped on the tire swing, and I pushed him. I forgot all about Nikki and her and Luke's disastrous "date." I was just relieved to see Luke acting more like himself.

After a while, our **verve diminished** of its own **accord** and we hopped onto adjacent swings. We just sat there, not swinging. With no activity to drown out the **morbid** thoughts, I worried that Luke's mood would slide back into **melancholia**. A part of me wanted to go back to playing, but my gut told me he kind of needed to talk.

"How do you remember her?" I asked.

"What do you mean?"

"You know, when you picture her with your mind's eye. Is she just like in the picture, smiling at the cat?"

"No. She's standing, like this . . ." Luke pulled himself off the swing. He balanced himself on his left foot, with his right foot

---

adumbration: symbol
artfully: skillfully
verve: vitality

diminished: lessened
accord: agreement

morbid: gloomy
melancholia: depression

pressed against his knee, like an ostrich. "And she's asking me questions about my life and really listening to my answers. She always stood like that, and it struck me as odd when I was a little kid because she was tall . . . like five ten."

"Really?"

"Yep."

"You couldn't tell from the picture," I said.

"Well, she was . . ." Luke's thoughts seemed to trail off with his words. Just as I began to worry that I was losing him, he spoke again. "You know what, that's not totally true." I pivoted in the swing so that I was facing him. "The way I remember her isn't quite that **majestic**. I mean, I remember her that way, too. But the way I usually see her is that last time, down at her place. She was thin as a rail from all the chemotherapy, but she still somehow managed to have a better **disposition** than the rest of us. She would sneak junk food behind Grandma and Grandpa's back and talk with me in the kitchen. The thing I remember most **vividly** was, one day, and this was only a few months ago, she was lying on her little portable bed in the living room, half-conscious from her pain medicine, and she looked over at me and said, 'Luke, those are just the nicest socks.' I had on these thick blue cotton socks with green and white stripes . . ." I could see he was losing it. "They really *are* great socks, and you could tell she wasn't kidding. She really liked those socks . . ."

With that, Luke just seemed to cave in on himself. I mean he was really bawling. I didn't know what to do—I'd never seen a guy cry like that. I was crying, too, and I reached over and patted him on the back. But it felt so weak, considering, and my heart ached at how much he was hurting. So I foot-pedaled in Luke's direction and put my arms around his neck. He swiveled and grabbed onto me, hugging me back. We sat there in our swings, holding each other so tightly I could feel his ribs against mine.

At first, I really was just **consoling** him, but then eventually he

majestic: grand **vividly:** clearly **consoling:** comforting
disposition: character

stopped crying, and so did I, and we didn't let go. I could hear the steady thump of his heart beating so close to mine and feel his soft breath on my neck. Suddenly there was this thing between us, something new. He pulled back from me, just a little, and looked into my eyes. A shudder passed through my whole body—I could feel myself being turned inside out, what that look did to me. Luke's face moved toward mine, until our lips nearly touched. My breath caught, and I felt dizzy, like if he wasn't holding me I'd fall. He inched closer, and my eyes fluttered closed, waiting . . .

A second later, I felt his lips touch—my cheek. "Thanks," he murmured, and then he let me go.

February 14: Valentine's Day

The universe really does have a great sense of humor. I mean, what's the deal with plopping Valentine's Day right in the middle of the most confusing time in the history of my barely existent romantic life?

I can't tell you how many times in the past two days I've replayed that scene on the swings with Luke in my mind. Was he about to kiss me? Did I just totally imagine it? Did I *want* him to kiss me? How could I, when I have a boyfriend like Jeremy who adores me and never pulls any of the stupid stunts Luke's capable of? Never drives me crazy like Luke does all the time. And when my own best friend is so hung up on the guy?

I told myself I'd just gotten carried away with the moment. That was typical of me. But today was about love, and that meant today was about *me and Jeremy*. I spent the afternoon decorating the school gym for the dance. You've never seen so much red and pink in all your life. At least, as Vice President, I was **allocated** a group of three **delegates** from Student Council whose job descriptions were to **accommodate** my every **whim**. We were to keep the tubs of punch full, take turns DJ-ing and emceeing, and watch the bathrooms for shady activity. Basically, hold down the fort.

I was too busy **toiling** to really enjoy the dance itself, but such is the life of a public servant. At least it went off without any major **glitches**. Of course no one had the guts to dance for the first hour, but that's par for the course. Not until the DJ put on that jam from last summer did a small, **eclectic** smattering of junior girls start

---

allocated: given
delegates: representatives
accommodate: provide for

whim: impulse
toiling: working

glitches: snags
eclectic: selective

moving. At first all the guys played the wall—scattered clumps of fidgeting head-nodders huddling around the **periphery**. But it didn't take long. The song changed to some cloying R&B **ballad**, and a few couples trickled out. Having broken the seal, hordes of guys flooded the floor. Jeremy even went out there—a **rarity**. Too bad it was the one night when I couldn't really be out there with him.

I noticed one guy who wasn't dancing. He was **circumnavigating** the floor, taller than the rest, accompanied by a girl with long, blond wavy hair. They turned in my direction, and my heart raced.

Luke.

He was walking right toward me, holding the girl's hand, and I frantically searched around for an escape route but realized it would have looked too obvious. So I waited, giving my best impression of a "Hey, what's up? I'm certainly not at all flustered at the sight of you" expression, and hoping it couldn't be easily mistaken for "Flustered! Flustered!"

When they reached me, he cupped his hand to my ear and said something that was **inaudible** over the **clamor**.

"WHAT?" I yelled back.

Luke leaned in closer and touched his lip to my ear, sending a chill down my spine. "We're not going to stay. I just wanted to say thanks, for the other day."

"You're welcome."

He stepped to the side and gestured at the blonde. "THIS IS BRITTANY!"

I'd kind of been hoping she would be a toad. Just so Nikki could feel better, I mean. But this girl was really something. Her blond waves cascaded down onto a worn-out t-shirt with "Bakersfield T-ball" stretched wide across her chest. Baggie camouflage pants on her long, lean legs. Momentarily blinded by her annoying **resplendence**, I didn't notice she was extending her hand.

"OH, HI!" We shook.

---

periphery: edges
ballad: song
rarity: uncommon circumstance

circumnavigating: going around
inaudible: too soft to hear

clamor: noise
resplendence: brilliance

"YEAH, SO WE JUST WANTED TO STOP BY AND SAY HI!" Luke yelled.

I waved and did a nervous little dance.

"OKAY, THEN!" Luke yelled. "HAVE A GOOD NIGHT!"

"YOU TOO!"

That was weird, I thought as they walked away. It was almost like a staged scene. *I think he just wanted me to* see *her.*

No, I was still stuck in paranoia mode. Had to get out of that. I gave my head a little shake, then glanced out at the dance floor, scanning for Nikki. There she was with her second choice date, Dennis Dalelio. Had she seen Luke and Brittany? I hoped not. She actually seemed to be having a good time with Dennis. Maybe pigs would start flying, and Nikki would actually be willing to consider dating someone who wasn't a total challenge.

I stayed to clean up after the dance, and Jeremy met me right outside the gym door with a **fervent** kiss and a look that said something was up his sleeve. "What?" I asked. "*What?*"

Jeremy pulled a key ring out of his front pocket and jingled it in my face.

"What's that?"

"Keys."

"Thanks, Captain Obvious," I said. "Keys to what?"

"To our hotel room."

My eyebrows flew up, and I gaped back at him. "Our what?" I guess it shouldn't have stunned me as much as it did. Jeremy had been dropping all these hints about how after the dance we'd have a special Valentine's Day celebration of our own. I'd figured that meant the usual—making out in his basement. But apparently he'd decided to get serious. The question was . . . did I feel the same way?

Jeremy's smile faltered. "Don't you think it's time?" he said. "I mean, we've been together *forever*, Fran. All the other guys and their girlfriends—"

---

fervent: intense

"Okay, stop right there," I interrupted. "Before you sound way too much like a bad cliché."

He rolled his eyes, then took a step closer and put his arms around my neck. "I just want to be with you, that's all," he said softly. And the thing is, I believed him. I knew he really did care about me, and he had been patient. And what was my problem, anyway? He was my boyfriend. This is what girlfriends and boyfriends did.

"Okay," I said.

"Really?" His whole face lit up, and it made me feel warm and cozy to see how happy he was.

"Yeah, let's go."

I called my parents and told them I was staying over at Nikki's, feeling a streak of rebellious excitement. We drove in separate cars to the Best Western just outside of town.

Jeremy and I walked into room 312, holding hands, not saying much. It was so quiet and **anonymous** in there, so **bereft** of atmosphere, that I felt myself losing my nerve almost immediately. In dreams, my first time usually occurred in some **fantastical solarium** on a bed **enshrouded** with white lace. Jeremy turned on the radio and the bathroom light. With all the built-up expectation, it was a little **unwieldy** getting started. Was I supposed to take my clothes off first, or wait?

We sat beside each other awkwardly on the bed. He leaned in and kissed the side of my neck in a way that he knows gets to me, then moved over to kiss me on the mouth. I closed my eyes, trying to relax, but it was no use. My whole body tensed up, and finally I couldn't take another second—I pushed him away, mumbling, "Stop, I'm sorry, stop."

"What happened?" he asked, opening his eyes.

I shrugged.

"What's that s'posed to mean?" Jeremy asked, **stupefied**. "Why did you push me away like that?"

---

anonymous: lacking identity   **solarium:** sunroom   **unwieldy:** awkward
bereft: lacking   **enshrouded:** enclosed   **stupefied:** amazed
fantastical: wonderful

"I don't know. I just can't."

He let out a frustrated sigh, then fell back on the bed. "So why'd you say okay, before?" he asked, his voice barely masking his annoyance.

"Jeremy, I'm sorry. I thought I could, but—I'm not ready."

Another deep sigh. Then . . . "Okay." He turned over and groaned into the pillow.

So much for our special Valentine's Day together.

February 22: George Washington's Birthday

We're stuck in that **stagnant** period of deep winter when days just sort of blend into each other. A week just rolled by, and I swear nothing happened. Wake up, hit snooze, get bundled up, go to class, eat, talk, do homework, eat, sleep. Repeat. My conversations with Nikki go back to the same focal point—me describing Brittany, in **minute** detail, since Nikki didn't in fact see her, and the fun time she had with Dennis wasn't enough to erase Luke from her brain. Luke, meanwhile, missed four days of school this past week because of the funeral and the wake, so Nikki isn't sure what's up with them. The only thing we know is that she definitely can't stop thinking about him.

Nikki isn't the only one. Because, see, I have a secret to admit. Something I didn't even write down when I was describing that whole miserable episode with Jeremy at the hotel.

God, I don't even know if I can make myself put it on paper now. No, I have to. If I get it out, maybe I'll realize it's crazy, and it'll be out of my system. Right? Right.

Okay. Deep breath. Here it is: When Jeremy and I were in that hotel room, the reason I couldn't go through with it wasn't just that I wasn't ready to have sex, even though I'm really not, and I know that now for sure. There was more. It was also that I didn't want to have sex *with Jeremy*. And I think I know why. I think it's because of something that changed between me and Luke on those swings.

I think I'm falling for Luke.

---

stagnant: stale   minute: precise

137

February 29:
Leap Day

Got a message on the machine from Luke saying he couldn't make tonight's makeup tutoring session because he had to work. I couldn't stop wondering—did he really have to work, or was he just afraid to see me? Was he feeling as mixed up about everything as I was? I know, I know, he has Nikki, and this Brittany chick, and who knows who else waiting in the wings. But I had Jeremy, and that wasn't stopping me from feeling like Luke and I had connected out there on the playground in a way that felt like nothing I'd ever experienced.

I was slowly driving myself insane. I had to know for sure if these feelings for Luke were real, or if maybe I was using them as an excuse somehow, to avoid getting too close to Jeremy. Or was I just overthinking everything?

I grabbed the phone and dialed Luke's number.

"Hello." Mrs. Barton's voice was hushed almost to the point of silence.

"Hi, Mrs. Barton. This is Francesca Castarelli."

"Oh, hi, Francesca. How are you?"

"Just fine. Actually, I was wondering how *you* were . . ."

"Oh, thank you. It's been hard over here, but we're getting through."

"I'm sorry," I said. "I'm sure you really miss her."

"Yes, very much," she agreed, sounding especially sad. "Thanks for coming to see Luke that day—it really seemed to help him."

It had? And he'd told her about my visit? I had to stop.

"He's not home right now, but I can tell him you called," she continued.

"Yeah, actually, that's why I was calling—he said something about working tonight, but I, um, I forgot the name of the place."

"Oh, no problem. It's called Jitterz, with a z."

"Coffee shop?" I guessed.

"Yes, exactly, over in West Hill."

"Great, thanks a lot. I hope you feel better soon, Mrs. Barton."

"Thanks Francesca. That's sweet of you. You take care too."

I hung up, making my decision. I could easily go to Jitterz under the **guise** of needing a new atmosphere to study in. Besides, the **notion** of getting homework done at a coffee shop appealed to me. And the added **impetus** of Luke Barton being my **obeisant** waiter-slave made driving out to West Hill not seem so bad.

I quickly slipped on my maroon-and-white Pumas and did my hair up in two ponytails, then threw my homework into my back-pack with **celerity**. I wasn't in the mood to **dawdle**. Nikki had also left a message, asking me to call when I got back from "hanging out with Jeremy," which was where I'd told her I'd be tonight instead of 'fessing up about the lesson. I didn't know what to say to her, exactly, but I'd think of something when I got back. Maybe by then, I'd know the real deal myself, finally.

Clumps of cars peppered the parking lot of the shopping center where Jitterz was located, and a bunch of kids my age were **loitering** in their vicinity. I figured maybe Noble Roman's Pizza was having some sort of two-for-one deep-dish deal. As it turned out, Jitterz itself was quite populated, with a cheery, well-lit **ambience**. The front section was filled with kids from school—mainly female. Was this some unexplored, underground *scene* going on in Columbus? It seemed highly **implausible**. Where was Luke? He was supposed to be behind the register, parroting that age-old **ingratiating** salutation: "May I help you?" Ah, well—so be it. I ordered a large chai tea latte and sat in the back, where I could plug in my laptop, people-watch, and work in relative peace.

---

guise: disguise
notion: idea
impetus: incentive
obeisant: submissive

celerity: speed
dawdle: hang around
loitering: loafing

ambience: atmosphere
implausible: unbelievable
ingratiating: flattering

But I wasn't much in the mood to do work. Something was in the air. I felt like writing down my thoughts instead. I'd been **besieged** by a steady **influx** of intense thoughts for the past few weeks. And it wasn't just my own situation. We just happened to be reading *Anna Karenina*, by Tolstoy, in English class, and the story had all these eerie parallels to my own life right now. Well, okay, maybe that was a little bit of a stretch, but Anna K. was all confused about which man she wanted to be with too.

Maybe I needed a break from anything too close to home. I decided to work on my vocabulary, instead, and write up a paragraph about my surroundings using words from my SAT prep book.

As an **inveterate** eavesdropper, I find the lives of perfect strangers way more **captivating** than they know. At the moment, I'm tuned to the wavelength of the **assemblage** of thirty-something women behind me. "Oh, my Gawd! Of course I saw her engagement ring! Was that not, like, the biggest, most **garish** rock you've ever seen!" "She only wants him for his money!" But my **capricious** ears tire quickly of their **cupidity** and tune into a different channel—the two **artisans** who just walked in the door . . .

I looked up. My heart thumped as I realized that one of the arty guys, the one with the guitar case strapped across his shoulder, was Luke. He noticed me **simultaneously** and flashed me a confused and rather **inscrutable** look.

"Hey," he said. "What's goin' on? Didn't you get my message?"

I opened my mouth to form the perfect, cool, and casual response. "Yep," is what came out. "I got it."

"So . . . how did you find me here?"

"Oh. I called you. Your mom told me where you were."

What was I doing? Hadn't my plan been to pretend this was purely a chance meeting? There went that. I'm a sucky liar.

Luke's eyes narrowed, and I realized that I sounded a little stalker-ish. My face reddened. He turned to the guy on his left, a

besieged: overtaken	**assemblage**: group	**artisans**: craftsmen
influx: flood	**garish**: gaudy	**simultaneously**: at the same
inveterate: habitual	**capricious**: fickle	time
captivating: appealing	**cupidity**: greed	**inscrutable**: unreadable

tattooed and yet somehow **urbane**-looking, dark-tanned, twenty-something guy with an easy smile.

"Francesca, this is Minh. Minh, this is Francesca."

"Men?" I asked.

"That works." We shook hands. Where did Luke find these people? This guy was so *not*-Columbus, so in his own world. He looked like a GQ model.

"Nice to meet you," I said, wondering what this guy was thinking of the weird stalker girl.

"Minh is one of three members of my jazz **collective**. I play flamenco guitar, and he plays drums. The other dude, who plays bass, is late. Again. Did you come here for our **gig**?"

"Gig? No," I said, and meant it. "I just came to study—and to, um, say hi. I thought you worked here as, like, a waiter or something."

"We make great background music," Minh said.

"All right, well, we need to go fuel up," Luke said.

I laughed. "Okay. Break a leg then."

"That's just for acting," Minh said.

I pretended to get back to my homework, scribbling thoughts to myself instead.

WE'RE BOTH BEING DODGY
NO, I'M BEING DODGY, HE'S BEING SKETCHED OUT
ALMOST KISS MEANT NOTHING

They got on stage and started warming up. I focused on his fingers massaging the strings. I knew he was a musician, but I'd never seen him play before. The bass player showed up, lugging his stuffed instrument case. They plucked around, did a little mini jam session and stopped. Luke leaned into the mike, which responded with the shrillest of sounds. A few girls up front hooted.

"Come in Houston," Luke said. "Testing one two three . . ."

---

urbane: elegant   **collective:** group

The same girls were now a giggling gaggle of chickenheads, puppets on his string.

"Sorry about that. But seriously now folks. We are The Lords. We want to thank you all for coming out tonight. And a big shout-out to Jitterz!"

We all clapped. The barista, a **convivial** brunette, curtsied at us from behind the **bulwark** of her glassed-in counter.

"We're gonna play something new tonight." Luke hushed the crowd with a delicate strum of his strings, letting the sound drift away. "I lost someone very close to me recently, and I wrote this song." He pulled away from the mike and took a dramatic swig of his water bottle. "It's called '**Moribund.**' "

With a title like that, you'd expect the song to be a bit heavy. But it was actually soft and **lilting**, a tribal drum line rolling along on guitar licks. I was **mesmerized**. I think everyone in there was. These guys were no wannabe hippie **charlatans**. They were talented musicians. Luke pressed his lips up to the mike. "**Lamenting** that you were with me before, but with me no more . . ." There was real emotion in the song. You could feel that it was real.

When the band took a break, Luke walked over and sat down across from me.

"Sorry about having to cancel the lesson again," he said. "They called us in when the scheduled performer canceled."

"Yeah, sure," I joked. "I know what's going on here—you're just trying to **sabotage** my chances so you can beat my score and take my spot at the Ivys."

Luke smirked. "That's me—cutthroat academic all the way."

I had to laugh at that image. Luke was one of those people who just happened to be smart. As arrogant as he was about his superior intellect, he didn't get caught up in all those contests in school over grades, class rankings, that stuff.

"So, I guess Brittany's back in California," I said, tracing the

convivial: sociable	**lilting:** rhythmic	**lamenting:** grieving
bulwark: wall	**mesmerized:** captivated	**sabotage:** damage
moribund: dying	**charlatans:** frauds	

pattern on the table with my finger.

"Yep, it was a short visit." He crossed his arms over his chest, leaning back in the chair. "We're just friends now, you know. Me and Brittany."

I coughed. Why was he telling me that? "Okay," I said, not sure how to respond. My gaze traveled over to the stage where he'd been playing. "So, the band—you guys are pretty decent."

"Decent, huh? Okay, I can work with that." He grinned back at me, and for a second, there was that *thing* between us again—that weird vibe that I couldn't even describe except that it made my neck feel warm and my palms start to sweat.

I guess it's why I didn't hear her footsteps, or see the familiar figure heading toward us in my **peripheral** vision. The first thing I heard was . . .

"Sorry to interrupt." Her voice was steely, cold, but also full of sadness that only someone who'd been her best friend for years could recognize.

I winced, knowing what her expression would look like before I turned to see it. But actually, it was even worse.

"Nikki—" I started.

"No, no, you guys are in the middle of something, no problem," she said quickly. I could tell her facial muscles were working overtime to hold off the waterworks.

"Nikki, it's not—"

"Don't worry, I covered for you with Jeremy," she practically spat out. "You know, when I tried his cell, looking for you, and he didn't have any idea where you were."

I went white, putting it all together. Didn't I say I was a sucky liar? Nikki had realized I'd fibbed about my plans with Jeremy, and she'd tracked me down here. That's why this looked so, so bad—like Luke and I had plotted some secret **rendezvous**.

"You might want to consider clueing him in, though," she added.

---

peripheral: within the outer part of the field (of vision) **rendezvous:** meeting

Her gaze moved to Luke. "Sometimes it's not the worst thing in the world to actually let someone know how you really feel."

With that, she turned and stalked out, ignoring my yells of "Nikki, wait!" and slamming the coffeehouse door shut behind her.

I dropped my face into my hands, rubbing my throbbing forehead. When I finally glanced up at Luke, he was avoiding my gaze, looking supremely uncomfortable, like he'd just been forced to eat spoiled brussel sprouts. A lot of them.

And that's when it sunk in. Luke didn't like me—I mean, at least, he didn't *like like* me. He'd been **vulnerable** that day on the playground. For God's sake, his aunt had just died. But he didn't want anything to do with all this girly melodrama. He just wanted to be friends, with me and with Nikki. And now I'd blown things with my best friend in the entire world over something that never was even anything.

---

vulnerable: open to attack

March 8: Working Women's Day

Nikki hasn't talked to me in a week. I've left like six bizillion messages on her machine. Finally, today, I decided I couldn't take it anymore. I **furtively** sneaked up on her at her locker and kind of pinned her there. "Hey," I said.

She looked at me, then banged her locker closed and turned to walk away. I followed. We were going to settle this. "Come on, Nik," I said. "You can't run away from me forever."

"Watch me."

I wracked my brain for something that would **assuage** her feelings. "I know it looked really bad, I do, but if you'd just let me explain, you'd see it's not like what you're thinking at all. See, we were originally supposed to have a tutoring session that night, but I didn't tell you because I knew you couldn't take hearing the sound of his name even, so I said I was out with Jeremy. And then Luke canceled the lesson at the last minute, so I went there to study, and his band was playing and   "

Nikki whirled around. "Just stop," she said. "I don't want to hear it anymore. Are you really that blind? You like him, Fran. You've always liked him."

"Just because I go to study at a place where he happens to be, doesn't mean I like him. It's a small town, that's all," I protested.

Nikki shook her head. "You are either in serious denial, or you're not the person I thought you were," she seethed. "The whole time, I'm trying to get this guy, sharing how I feel about him with you, and

---

furtively: secretly   assuage: ease

147

you're stealing him from under my nose. You and Luke probably got a good laugh out of it."

My mouth dropped open. "Nikki, how could you say that? You make it sound like—like I'm **colluding** with him against you. You know me better than that."

"I thought I knew you. Look, do what you want, Francesca. Just do it somewhere else, away from me." She picked up her pace. "And quit following me."

colluding: scheming

March 15: The Ides of March

I was forced to **prevaricate** to get a day off school today. I claimed PMS complications, even though mine won't come until late next week. It's quite possible that I'm losing my mind.

The only person who still wants to be around me is Jeremy, and I feel so guilty around him, even though I never actually did anything with Luke. But I feel ten times worse about Nikki. She's right—I can argue facts with her, and on paper I didn't do anything wrong. But I did lie to her, and I did have some mixed up feelings about the guy she's been pining after for months now.

But the thing is, *she's* the one who sort of pushed us together in the first place, with that whole elaborate tutoring plan. Am I evil for thinking about that? I know I have to stay away from him now—I know best friends come first, and I broke that rule. But I also can't help feeling like all of this is a little bit her fault. Just a little bit. Because as usual, she pulled me into one of her wacky schemes, and this time it had a little unintended **consequence** that I really couldn't prevent.

My horoscope today read, "You are not being honest with your heart." All I do is mope around in a tragically **lackluster** fashion, watching bad movies and reading *Anna Karenina*. I feel more and more like I can relate to Anna's **predicament**. The guy she really wants couldn't be more inconvenient. She's at odds with the society around her, and she's bound to lose in the end. I wonder what'll happen to her.

Mom came up to check on me this afternoon. She called through

---

prevaricate: lie   lackluster: unimpressive   predicament: dilemma
consequence: result

the door and asked if I wanted to talk. I didn't. She said she'd feel a lot better if I would let her in. I did. As it turned out, I did want to talk. I told her the whole story, unabridged, from alpha to omega. I even used episodes from *Anna Karenina* as instructional **metaphors** so Mom could relate to my dilemma.

"So what're you going to do?" Mom asked. "Break up with Jeremy and go out with Luke?"

"I can't."

"Stay with Jeremy and do nothing about Luke?"

"Can't do that either."

"Well I say you drop them both and make up with Nikki. That's the most important thing. Never let a guy **wreak havoc** on your friendships with your girlfriends."

"You're probably right," I said. "But I just hope it's not too late."

---

metaphors: comparisons   **wreak:** inflict   **havoc:** chaos

I couldn't stand it anymore. No longer could I **languish** alone with my thoughts, my best friend hating me, too overcome by the **inertia** of self-hate to sleep, do homework, or function socially. A decisive and valiant step had to be taken.

Such was the misguided logic in place when I hopped into my cute little Saturn and drove to Jitterz tonight, looking for Luke himself. I tried to time my entrance perfectly with the end of his set. The plan backfired though, because when I got there, the place was almost empty. I asked a waitress, who was sweeping up, if The Lords had played there.

"Finished up about a half hour ago. They all left. Except Luke, of course. He's out back with Ol' Buckethead."

"Who?"

"Our dishwasher."

"Oh. Can I see him? It's kind of an emergency."

"Well I'm not supposed to take customers through the back offices."

"Pleeease," I **importuned.**

"I guess it wouldn't hurt anything. The owners aren't around. Follow me . . ." She lifted up the counter and ushered me back. We walked past an office space, which couldn't have been more **immaculate.**

"It's right through that door," she said. "And tell those guys that I'm leaving in another fifteen minutes, so it's about time for them to leave."

---

languish: suffer   importuned: pestered   immaculate: spotless
inertia: sluggishness

"Got it. Thanks."

I opened the door and saw Luke and an elderly **swarthy** man with graying hair, sitting across from each other on milk crates, backs propped against opposing dumpsters. This guy was presumably "Buckethead," though nothing about the shape of his head warranted such an **epithet**.

Luke glanced up and saw me, and I tried to judge his reaction but couldn't really decipher anything from his poker face.

"Hi," I said. "Um, Luke, I need to talk to you."

"Go ahead. Shoot."

"Could we maybe have a little privacy?"

Luke nodded. "If you'll excuse me," he said to the older guy. He pulled himself off the milk crate, slowly. "Where were you thinking of going?"

"Right over there, I guess." I pointed to behind the Dumpster.

"Okay."

I walked around the Dumpster until we were out of earshot, then turned to him.

"I just have to get this out, okay?"

"Okay," he said, smiling in that condescending way of his. At least that made what I had to do easier.

"We can't hang out, ever again," I said.

Luke chuckled. "That's what you came here to say?"

"My best friend hates me, and my boyfriend's totally suspicious."

"And this is *my* problem?"

The casual way that he said it enraged me. "I guess it's not then. If you don't care."

"Did I say that? I'm just not sure why you have to jump every time someone in your life says the word."

I drew in a deep breath. "Maybe you don't understand what it means to have an actual *commitment* to someone," I began, "but when people are counting on me, I take that seriously."

---

swarthy: of dark   epithet: nickname
complexion

Luke shrugged. "All right then, fine."

"Fine?"

"Yeah, if we can't see each other any more, so be it. What am I supposed to do?"

I stared back at him, feeling angrier by the second. "Nothing, I guess," I said. "You're good at that, right? Feeling nothing?"

I knew I wasn't making any sense—he was agreeing to what I asked for, and I was furious at him for it. But couldn't he show he cared, just a little?

"Hold on," Luke said. "If you want to show up here and make a big production out of how we can't talk anymore, go ahead. But you can stop with all the cuts, okay? What about you? You are the most self-absorbed, **solipsistic** human I've ever met. And I know you don't know what that means, so you'll just have to look it up when you get home . . ." (True.) "You think the world only exists in your head, from your perspective. But guess what? I've had some *real* problems lately, from *my* perspective, and I don't have time to **kowtow** to you and whatever **overwrought** issues you've fabricated in your little head."

"Oh," I said, tears springing to my eyes. "I see."

"But it sure has been a pleasure knowing you." Luke extended his hand for a final, sarcastic shake. I shook my head instead. "Have a nice life," he added.

"Fine!" I yelled.

"Fine!" Luke parroted.

I stomped past the Dumpster, wondering where a handy door to slam was when you needed it.

---

solipsistic: self-centered   **kowtow**: bow down to   **overwrought**: exaggerated

Jeremy is the only string of hope I have left, and even our relationship feels **tenuous**. Which is why I went out of my way to smother him with affection today.

I even told him I was ready to *do it*, and I wasn't playing around this time. Luke had my head all messed up, but now I know Jeremy's the one I belong with, and I need to do this to prove I'm serious.

Jeremy hedged at first, worried I wasn't really ready, but ultimately **relented** when I stuck to my story. He said his parents were going up to Indy for a play on the twenty-first, in three days, so that would be perfect. That'd be great, I told him, and meant it wholeheartedly. So there you have it, the official word on my virginity: T minus three and counting.

tenuous: shaky   relented: yielded

March 19

Mom came up to my room tonight, as a sort of follow-up visit to the heart-to-heart we had the other night. She wanted to know if I had made peace with Nikki. I hadn't.

"Well, maybe *this* will **alleviate** her anger." Mom pulled an envelope from behind her back.

"What's this?" I asked, ripping it open. It had five tickets, from Indy to Ft. Myers Airport, for next week . . . spring break! "Oh, thank you, Mom!" I screeched, throwing my arms around her neck.

"The extra ticket in there is for Nikki," she said. "And your father and I reserved a separate room for you two, to give you some time together."

"Mom, you're amazing," I gushed.

Nikki has to forgive me now, right?

alleviate: lessen

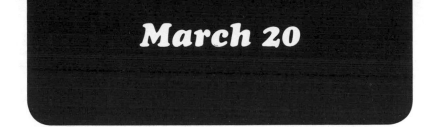

I emailed Nikki three times. The first time, I said I had a surprise for her. The second time, I said it was an emergency, and she had to contact me immediately. The third time, I couldn't hold it in anymore. I told her the whole deal—that my parents had purchased tickets and a hotel room for both of us down in Florida. She finally replied: "That's sweet of your parents. But I've already got plans. I'm going to Jamaica with my parents."

March 21: Naw Ruz (Persian New Year)

I was totally prepared. I really was. Jeremy picked me up at home. We went to Applebee's for dinner. It went fine, though my Chicken Cobb Salad was more filling than I'd expected and left me feeling less than sexy. And then, there was the fact that Jeremy kept looking at his watch. He snarfed down his food and, even though I was less than half-finished with my salad, asked for the check. We had to hurry up, he said, or we would "miss our window."

He drove like a banshee to his place. We dashed up to his room. We started kissing, with good old Les Nubians playing on the stereo. And then it happened, again. I felt terrible when it hit me, that I still couldn't go through with this. It was cruel to Jeremy, I knew. But that wasn't enough to make this huge, gigantic mistake worth it. You can never have another first time, you know?

"Man!" Jeremy said, sensing my withdrawal. "What's wrong this time?"

I bit my lip. What was wrong . . . that I still couldn't get Luke off my brain? That, if I would just be honest with myself, for once, I would know I'd only decided to do this as a way to forget about Luke and stop feeling guilty with Jeremy?

"Maybe we should wait until after spring break," I said.

"What? Are you *kidding* me? After you promised me, again? I'm sorry, but you just can't do this to me, Fran. I asked you if you were sure, remember? You said you were. You swore you were."

I flinched. "I know. I'm so sorry. But the first time has to feel right. And this just doesn't."

Jeremy turned away, buttoning up his shirt. "That's it. I can't take it anymore. With you. With us. I think it's time we took a break."

"Whoa," I said. "You're gonna break up with me because I won't have sex with you?"

"It's not just that, Francesca. It's the way you've led me on, and all the Luke stuff . . . I don't even feel like you *like* me. You're just using me for . . ."

"*I'm* using *you*? Interesting. What am I using you for?"

"I don't know. As a prop. It's like I'm another notch on your stick or something. You know, Vice President. Soccer Captain. Girlfriend of Jeremy. I feel like you'd put me on your college application if you thought it would help you out."

"Wow," I said. "Well, it's good to know how you *really* feel."

Jeremy let out a frustrated groan. "That came out wrong," he said. "It's not like that."

"So then . . . what's it like?"

Jeremy raked his hand through his hair. He sat back down on the bed and faced me. "Actually, what I was trying to say to you . . . what I've been wanting to say is . . . I love you."

"*What?*"

"I said, I love you." Jeremy looked satisfied with himself, for the **valor** it took to get this out. But somehow, just like everything else tonight, it didn't feel right. See, I had thought about those three words in relation to him. I had thought about whether we'd say them, and how, and how you would have to feel right before you knew it was time to say them. I had even felt close to saying it myself. But I wasn't sure anymore, and, regardless, this was *not* the right moment.

"Did you not hear me?" he repeated. "I said I love you."

"I heard you."

"And?"

"And . . ."

---

valor: courage

Jeremy's eyes flashed. "Forget it." He said. "Forget I said anything."

"What do you want me to do?" I **entreated** him. "Just a second ago, you wanted to break up. You said I was superficial and I was using you for my college application, and now you're telling me you love me? You can't keep **vacillating** like that."

"Forget it," he repeated.

"No, Jeremy, wait—I mean, the truth is . . . I think I love you too," I forced out, desperate to stop this situation from spinning further out of control.

"Oh, my God, Fran. You *think* you love me? That's even worse than not saying it at all. I don't need your pity. I was right the first time—it's time to take a break."

"So now we're breaking up?"

"Taking a break," Jeremy corrected.

The emerging possibility that he wasn't kidding, that I could, within the next few seconds, become the former girlfriend of Jeremy Malone, suddenly hit me. But I wasn't exactly grief-stricken. Just stunned. It was crazy the way you could be one thing one second and something else the next. How fast life could change so drastically. "You really mean that?" I asked.

"Uh huh."

"All right, then. I guess that's that."

"I guess *so*. I should probably drive you home now, before my parents get here."

Up to this point, I was convinced that whatever damage I'd just **incurred** was still reversible. It was a fight, and maybe we'd take a break, but not for long. But the fact that he wanted me to leave *now*, before his parents got home, seemed extra final.

"I'll walk," I said, knowing it would either be the longest drive of my life, or we'd get back together. Right now I wanted neither.

"Don't be stupid. It's like a half-hour walk. I'll drive you."

"No, really. Thanks, but I'll walk."

---

entreated: begged   **vacillating:** wavering   **incurred:** brought on oneself

March 25: Spring Break

Why didn't anyone tell me Anna Karenina *dies*? She actually throws herself onto train tracks. That is seriously messed up. And really not helping matters right now.

It's just like me to pick spring break for the onset of severe, **acute** depression. The enormity of what has **transpired** in the last week hit me full-throttle on the plane ride. Nikki thinks I'm a traitor. Jeremy thinks I'm a tease and a user. Luke thinks I'm self-absorbed. And right now, I'm pretty sure I **accede** with all three of them.

So just because I'm at the beach doesn't mean I'm feeling particularly **buoyant**. I have spent my first three days here sleeping, watching TV, and laying out by the pool with my book. At around noon each day, groups of college kids, mainly guys, start coming by. They **boisterously** yell back and forth. I feel them looking at me, but they never approach. I'm hoping this can be **ascribed** to the depressed vibe I'm giving off, as opposed to me just being straight-up butt ugly.

My parents check on me, to give me reassuring pats. They take me out to dinner and grill me about why I'm so **sullen**. But talking about it just makes it worse, so I don't. I've cried a handful of times, but for the most part I'm just numb. Being **reclusive** is weird like that. After a while, when no one can hear you cry, you just dry up. Last night, I finished reading *Anna Karenina*. Aside from being ticked off at the frustrating ending, I decided that the story is a decent metaphor for how I feel—like I'm sliding down a long slope, powerless, toward some unforeseen tragedy.

---

acute: sharp
transpired: happened
accede: agree

buoyant: cheerful
boisterously: energetically
ascribed: attributed

sullen: grim
reclusive: solitary

This morning, however, I woke up and the cloud had lifted somewhat. I stopped fixating on the friends I'd **estranged**. I got up, took a shower and put on my bathing suit. I went down to the pool again, but this time I went without a book, hoping, for the first time in days, to interact with the world. Unfortunately, it was only half-past-seven, so I was the only one there except a **portly** old man who was cleaning the pool.

I watched him sweep a long pole across the surface of the water, whistling to himself. For most people (myself included), this would be the most boring no-brainer of a job you could ever imagine. But this guy did it with such **élan**—skipping around the pool's **perimeter**, smiling even as he cleaned the gook from the drains with his bare hands. I had never seen such a **commendable** attitude. I was sure that, if you pried, this guy, like the rest of us, could find reasons to despair. He just chose not to. It reminded me of a quote I'd once read by Martin Luther King, Jr.: "If you're a street sweeper, be the Michelangelo of street sweepers."

After a bit, the man walked up to me. I thought I'd been watching him **clandestinely**, without him noticing, but I should've known better. He was the type who saw things.

"Excuse if I am nosy, miss," he said in broken English. "And please don't take the offense . . ."

I smiled an easy smile to let him know I wouldn't.

"But can you say how it is that such a beautiful young woman is down here all alone?"

I know. Sounds like a **trite** Dirty Old Man line. But there was something about his delivery, his whole bearing, that didn't make it seem that way. "You're sweet," I said. I was even blushing a little.

"No, really, I mean it. Where I come from, a young woman like you would be swarmed."

"Where are you from?" I asked.

"I am from Greece." He said it with such pride. "A little village,

---

estranged: alienated   **perimeter:** outside edge   **clandestinely:** secretly
portly: stout   **commendable:** admirable   **trite:** stale, commonplace
élan: flair

in the south part. If you were there, I tell you, you would not walk ten feet without guys coming . . . from everywhere!" He laughed a few happy snorts.

"That sounds nice," I said.

"Yes. But really, this I don't understand. What is wrong with American men? Where are they?"

"Asleep, I guess. It's pretty early."

"But that is not excuse! I have seen you here before, in the day, and where are they?"

I shrugged. He shrugged.

"I cannot understand," he said.

"To be honest, I don't think it's entirely their fault. I'm kind of alone by choice."

"Oh," he said, stunned. "I see. But *why*?"

"Sometimes guys are more trouble than they're worth," I said.

"Oh, no, no . . ." He started waving his hands around, as if swatting at an invisible bee. "This will not do. This is not life."

"Excuse me?"

"You read, yes? You are reader?"

"Mm hmm."

"I will tell you something from my favorite book. You have heard of the *Zorba the Greek*, by Kazantzakis?"

"I think so."

"In that book, he writes something that I don't forget . . ." He took a step back and raised two fingers in front of his face, like a man about to say something noteworthy. "He says, 'To live. Do you know what that means? To go out and look for trouble!'" He let out a big, bellowing laugh, then looked at me with his piercing brown eyes. "You understand?"

"I think so," I said. "Yeah, I understand. I'm good at trouble."

"That's good. Remember that. It is something to know, okay?"

"Okay."

"Now I must go. I am not to talk to the swimmers. The boss, he knows how I love to talk. I will see you, yes? You will remember me?"

"Of course I will. How could I forget you?"

"That's good. Everyone wants to be remembered."

"What is your name?" I asked.

"I am Stavros. And you are called?"

"Francesca."

"Ah, Francesca! What a beautiful name! A beautiful name for a beautiful girl to start off a beautiful day! Have the _best_ day, Francesca! Go out and look for trouble!" With that, his closing line, Stavros grabbed his pool supplies and walked away.

March 27

Today there was a guy at the pool. A **plenitude** of them, actually, but only one that mattered. I had been watching him for a while, and not just because he was exceedingly cute—bright blue eyes, a tanned, carved-up bod straight off the cover of *Men's Fitness*, a cowlick on the right side of his forehead. I was utterly riveted, also because of something he did.

They were throwing a football, he and his friends, from the shallow end to the deep end, to the hot tub, and into the arms of whoever would call out "Hit me!" before running toward the pool's edge for a spectacular, highlights-reel-style diving catch. But this guy—the one I'm talking about—was the only one who noticed two younger boys, no older than eight, splashing around and watching the whole scene with wide-eyed admiration.

"You wanna play too?" the guy said to the younger boys. They were too **diffident** to answer, but you could see that they did. He threw the ball to one of them, who fumbled it in the water, then dog-paddled after it as quick as he could and threw it back. Then the guy—my guy—threw it to the other kid, who caught it and threw it back.

"Nice toss," My guy said.

"Yo, man," one of his buddies in the hot tub said. "You're jackin' up the game. Throw the ball over here."

"Shut up!" my guy said. "Chill out."

He passed it a few more times with the younger kids, then threw the ball over to his hot-tub buddies. That's when I knew I had to

---

plenitude: abundance   diffident: timid

169

be **plucky** and try to talk to him. *Go out and look for trouble.* The problem was, there was no way to get close to him without making an idiot of myself. I couldn't just dive in there and kind of swim around in his vicinity. And even if, by some divine **infusion** of courage, I could summon up a smooth conversation-starter, I would be instantly crushed by a chorus of oohs and ahhhs from all his primate buddies.

It was then that an idea hit me and came to full blossom in my head. I opened the copy of *Zorba the Greek* that I'd bought the day before at the local bookstore. There were a couple blank pages at the end of the book. I ripped one out and, with the pen that I'd been bringing to the pool daily but, until this moment, had never actually used, I wrote out the stupidest message you've ever read. I promptly **jettisoned** that message and wrote the following on the scrap that remained:

Francesca   Room 312

Not bad. What it lacked in specificity, it made up for in mystery. Could seem a little slutty if it fell into the wrong hands. But I knew, or felt strongly, that his hands were not the wrong ones. It was just a matter of getting them there. When I saw him swimming toward the ladder, I realized opportunity was about to knock. I gathered up all my stuff and walked toward the projected point of contact. My timing couldn't have been more precise. Just as his water-glazed body rose up from the ladder, I "accidentally" bumped into him.

"Oh. Excuse me," he said.

I said nothing. I held a tiny piece of paper up for him to see, flashed a slight smile and handed it to him. Using every shred of **restraint** of which I am capable, I didn't sprint out of there, but **sauntered** away with calm, measured steps.

plucky: gutsy   ettisoned: abandoned   sauntered: strolled
infusion: outpouring   restraint: self-control

March 28

No sight of him yet. I am beginning to doubt the Greek man's **sagacious** advice, or at least my interpretation of it. I'm 130 pages into *Zorba the Greek*, and I'm grooving on it, though Zorba's having a better go of it than I am. I've played so many games of Boggle that I actually **attained** the Boggle Holy Grail: an eight-letter, eleven-point word. The word was *epitomes*—totally underused word. As in: If there were two of me, both of us would be the epitomes of sheer idiocy if we kept waiting around for this guy to show up. Okay, fine, **epitome** really isn't plural, because there's only one epitome of something—but I think I deserved a little slide on that one after everything I've been through lately.

Finally, my **forbearance** pushed to the breaking point, I made the executive decision to go with my parents to the manatee park. The manatee park is next to this big electricity plant. It's almost like a *Simpsons* episode. The manatees come to huddle in the warm glow of the plant's **incandescence**, which could be **discomfiting** if you think too hard about it. We walked out onto a wooden bridge and watched these overgrown slugs with mammalian facial features float up to the surface to sniff for air.

We were all on the hunt for them. When someone pointed—"Hey look!"—the rest of us would run over to that spot to coo at this snorting sea cow. It made you feel good that these **benevolent behemoths** were **extant**, swimming around, tending to their young and gnawing marine grasses. It made you want to kiss their **cleft** chins and nuzzle up to their whiskered snouts. The Everglades had

---

sagacious: wise
attained: achieved
epitome: ideal
forbearance: patience

incandescence: radiance
discomfiting: unsettling
benevolent: noble
behemoths: mighty animals

extant: existing
cleft: cracked

shrunken, sure, and the churn of boat propellers had **lacerated** their backsides (or so I read on a sign posted on the bridge describing the life cycle of the manatee), but none of it could **deter** the manatees from this dose of warm, wet love. These **resilient** beasts had the same recipe for comfort as us **terrestrial** mammals: a **distended** belly and some warm, cozy love.

lacerated: slashed   **resilient:** durable   **distended:** swollen
deter: discourage   **terrestrial:** earthly

He came.

My heart shot up through my esophagus when I heard the knock. The first thing he said was, where had I been? He had stopped by three times already, yesterday afternoon and once in the evening. (Stupid manatees!) He said he even talked to the grouchy **dotard** next door. He told me his name: Connor. I was Francesca, I said, barely holding it together. Thank God he was wearing a shirt, or I would've been fidgeting like a freak not to gawk at him. I told him straight up that if he thought I was some **ingénue** and his designs were purely **amorous**, then we should just shake and say bye now. I was just out for an innocent, friendly adventure. He said that was good to hear because he was dating someone back at school anyway.

We went out to walk and talk on the beach. Connor's official deal was dreamy-college-athlete-frat-boy-Communications-major. He played lacrosse at Virginia, a fact gathered by the insignia and number on his orange baggy shorts.

"What exactly do you study as a Communications major?" I asked.

"I know. It sounds ridiculous, right? It's, like, are they teaching me how to talk on the phone or what? I mean, from the sound of it, I could be working toward my degree right now."

I laughed. "Because we're communicating."

"Exactly. So Francesca, tell me, what do you think about my communication skills? Pretty awesome, huh? What grade would you give me?"

---

dotard: old person   **ingénue:** naïve young girl   **amorous:** interested in love (erotic)

"On your communication skills?" I asked.

"Yeah. Go ahead. Hit me."

"I don't know. B-plus?"

"B-plus!" Connor mock-yelled. "That sucks! That's the worst grade of all, 'cause it's not quite an A!"

"A-minus?" I squeaked.

We laughed. When it **subsided**, I asked, "So, seriously, what does that mean? What do you do with a Communications major? You know, as, like, a **vocation**?"

"Oooh. That one. Toughie. Hmm. To be honest, that's where we run into a little bit of a gray area."

"How gray?"

"Charcoal."

"You stole that line from Chevy Chase," I **recriminated**.

"You're right," he said. "From *Fletch*. I'm impressed you know that. You an eighties movie buff or something?"

"Yeah, sort of."

"Cool. Me too. You know, that wouldn't be such a bad thing either. Maybe I'll go to Hollywood and become an actor, like Chevy."

"So Communications majors become actors?"

"They can," Connor said. "Lots of us go into journalism. I was thinking about the game show host route. What do you think?"

I looked at him, trying to see if he was joking. After a second he started to laugh, and I laughed too. This was how all our conversations went—lots of talking nonsense and laughing at it. His self-**deprecating** sense of humor kept me in stitches. He said he couldn't wait for me to go out partying with him that night, obviously **oblivious** to the fact that I was down there with my parents. No reason to tell him, really. It was enough to admit that I was in high school, even though I somehow turned into a senior who would be **matriculating** at Northwestern in the fall. (Which wasn't a total lie. I *was* thinking of applying there.)

---

subsided: died down
vocation: career or profession

recriminated: accused
deprecating: insulting
oblivious: unaware

matriculating: beginning school

For the rest of the day, I felt lighter than I had in weeks. It felt nice to take a little break from hating myself and feeling incessantly guilty. I walked into town to buy myself a shirt suitable for being seen among the "college crowd." I **acquired** a SnoKone and ended up with a purple ring around my lips, just like back in the day. Read a few more pages of my novel out on the patio and ate dinner with my parents and Rico.

Later, I went down to Connor's apartment at around ten. The guys staying there—Steve, Ryan, Mike, and Watts—were all **gregarious** and nice-looking, with their baseball caps worn in the exact same way. After hanging out in their apartment for a while, we drove to some garishly decorated dance club that was fairly **burgeoning** with **carousing** spring-breakers. Connor showed his gentlemanly side by paying my ten-dollar cover charge.

It was funny. Seemed like the second you had a guy-friend around, guys would start coming out of the woodwork. I got hit on by a **plethora** of guys, most of whom didn't even bother to **utilize** come-on lines. Luckily, my crew of Virginia lacrosse boys **emancipated** me each time, boldly stepping in between the most recent **interloper** and me.

Connor and I didn't get to talk as much as I'd hoped, because the place was just too loud. But we danced like fools. I was psyched to see that he had enough rhythm to dance respectably to hip hop music. At around four in the morning, Connor asked if I was ready to split.

Never in my life had I had the option to take a guy back to "my place"—a place in which my parents weren't. It felt cool and mature, but on the other hand, inviting Connor over, especially after my **brazen** pool-side introduction, seemed like the type of courtesy that could be easily misinterpreted. So instead we went for another walk on the beach, talking some more about our lives and even about his girlfriend and my ex, Jeremy. He said Jeremy didn't deserve me, and

acquired: bought	**carousing:** partying	**emancipated:** liberated
gregarious: outgoing	**plethora:** excess	**interloper:** intruder
burgeoning: bursting	**utilize:** use	**brazen:** bold

that I'd find someone else who did. I couldn't believe it when the sun started to come up—the night had flown by. Connor walked me back to my room and said goodbye.

"I guess this is it," he said when we stopped in front of my door. "It was cool meeting you, Francesca. Wish I'd met you earlier."

"Me too," I said. We hugged goodbye, and he gave me a quick kiss on the cheek.

And yes, it reminded me of a certain someone whose name starts with the letter "L," okay? But we're not going there right now.

Looking back (I'm on the plane ride home now), that whole day and night with Connor was really perfect, probably because it was also so **transient**. We had just enough time together to know that we liked each other, and not long enough to start figuring out we didn't. Stavros was right about looking for trouble. Unfortunately, as soon as I get back, I have to do the exact opposite—**extricate** myself from the trouble I've caused. But for now, it's time to put my tray table up, lean my seat back, and catch some sleep.

transient: brief   extricate: remove

April 1: April Fool's Day

On the plane ride back, I thought a lot about Nikki. I knew that if we were ever going to **reconcile**, drastic measures were needed. I had a few tricks left in my **arsenal** that might get us talking again. Connor and I had done a quick analysis of all our favorite eighties movies on our second walk on the beach, and thinking about *Say Anything*—the one where adorable John Cusack does everything he can to win over Ione Sky—gave me an idea.

So last night, I threw on some clothes, grabbed my boom box and sped over to Nikki's house. Walked around to the back of their house, bribing Duffy, their golden retriever, with some Snausages I'd brought for this express purpose. Pulled the cassette tape out of my pocket, popped it in the deck, and pressed play. The music was so loud—such an **egregious** interruption to the neighborhood's **sedateness**—that I had the urge to run away. But I didn't. I stood my ground and even furthered my Cusack-ness by lifting the boom box over my head.

"Don't cryyyy out louuuud! Just reach deep inside, and learn how to hide your feelings . . ."

Nikki and I used to do karaoke performances to this song, for an audience of stuffed animals. We wore Sunday School dresses and used spoons as microphones. Just as lights started flipping on at the next-door-neighbor's, Nikki lifted her window.

"Turn that off!" she yelled. "What's wrong with you?"

"Are you coming down to talk?" I asked.

"No!"

---

reconcile: reunite, restore to friendship   **arsenal:** weapons storehouse   **egregious:** conspicuous   **sedateness:** calm

"Then I won't turn it off . . . *Don't cryyyy out louuuud!*"

"I should call the cops on you."

"Double-dog dare you," I said.

"Turn that off, Fran! My parents are gonna kill you."

"Are you coming down?" I beckoned.

"All right, all right. Just turn that thing off."

In a matter of minutes, Nikki was right out there in the yard with me. I wanted to run up and hug her, but I knew that wasn't how the old foot-in-the-door technique worked. It would take some patience to seal the deal. Without saying a word, Nikki walked past me and sat down on the bench back by the shrubbery.

"Thanks for coming out," I said. "How was Jamaica?"

"It was fine," she said brusquely. "Start talking."

"I'm so sorry, Nikki," I said. "Sorrier than the sorriest sorry, really I am. Please forgive me."

"For what?" Nikki crossed her arms and stared straight ahead.

"For, um, for making you so upset, when you didn't understand what was—"

Nikki stood up and looked poised to walk away.

"Okay!" I said. "That's not what I meant."

She sat back down.

"I guess what I'm sorry for is that I wasn't always totally honest with you about Luke."

"You *guess*?"

"Basically, yeah. I mean, nothing really ever happened between us. We never *did* anything. But—but we almost did."

Nikki cringed. "When?" she asked.

"After his aunt died. He started to cry, so I hugged him. And then there was this moment, and it did seem like he was going to kiss me, but he ended up just kissing me on the cheek instead."

She looked away, then back. "Okay. You know what—I don't want to hear this. Just tell me, do you like him?"

I let out a shaky breath. There it was, the million-dollar question. I hadn't said it out loud, ever. I've barely even written it in here!

"I guess I kind of do." I looked at her, my heart aching. "Do you hate me now?"

She was silent for just about the longest moment in the history of time. "No," she finally said, so softly I could barely hear. "At least you can admit it now. That was the worst part, feeling like you were lying to me."

I wanted so badly to give her a big hug. "I've missed you so much, Nikki. Over break, every time I thought about you I would get so **despondent.**"

"Yeah, me too." She sighed. "So what are you going to do about Jeremy?"

I blinked, confused. Then I realized that for the first time in forever, Nikki was in the dark about a huge development in my life. "I forgot you didn't know," I said. "Jeremy and I broke up."

"Really? For good?"

"Well, I think it was officially labeled a break. But we'll see."

"Why? Because of Luke?"

"No," I said. "Because I wouldn't have sex with him."

"Oh. Well, I'm sorry then. That sucks."

Her slight note of sympathy just made me hungry for more. "But you know what? If I lose Jeremy, I do. But you . . . that I couldn't handle. And I couldn't wait until tomorrow. Which is why I came over here to play our song and make up."

"You're crazy." She let a little laugh escape, a faint glimmer of hope.

"Maybe so, but losing you would make me certifiably, stark raving mad."

"I doubt that."

"Please, please take me back, Nikki. You are everything to me, the one and only **confidante** I ever want and need."

---

despondent: depressed   **confidante:** friend entrusted with secrets

"Easy on the cheese," she said.

"So, am I forgiven then?" I asked.

"You're not only forgiven, but I'm officially dropping out of the Luke race. He's yours."

"No. You don't have to do that. It would probably be best for me to be alone for—"

Nikki put her hand on my leg. "Trust me, Francesca. I don't want him anymore. The truth is, I think I was over him a while ago. It was more like an ego thing, you know? It drove me crazy that *he* didn't want *me*."

I raised my eyebrows. "Since when are you so self-aware?" I asked.

She bit back a smile. "Well . . . there's something new on my end, too," she admitted.

"What is it? Spill!" I demanded.

She giggled, then leaned in closer, lowering her voice. "Turns out, Dennis Dalelio's family went to Jamaica for spring break too," she said, her eyes sparkling. "Same hotel as us and everything."

"Oh my God—so, wait, are you guys together?"

She shrugged. "We'll see," she said. "There was definite kissage happening, I'll say that much."

I almost shrieked, then clapped my hand over my mouth as I remembered we were in Nikki's garden in the middle of the night.

"So the point is, I think you should just go for Luke," Nikki said. "Really."

I frowned. "I'm happy for you and Dennis, Nik," I said, "and it's really nice of you to be okay about the me and Luke thing. But honestly, I don't think it's happening anyway. After we fought, before Jeremy broke up with me, I went to see Luke at Jitterz and kind of made a big stupid scene. I told him I couldn't see him anymore, at all."

Nikki winced. "Because of me?" she said.

I nodded. "Yeah, because of you, and Jeremy. I just thought it was the right thing to do. But I said everything all wrong, and I don't even think it matters because it doesn't seem like Luke's into me either."

"I'm sorry," Nikki said, putting her arm around me. "I really am."

I forced a smile, pushing Luke out of my mind. "It's okay. You know why? Because as long as I have you back, I don't need any of those guys."

April 9: Good Friday

During my fifteen-minute break at work today, I went out to my car, where I knew a bag of delicious spicy nacho Doritos were waiting for me. While unlocking the door, I saw a shock of color that was definitively *not* Doritos. A huge bouquet of flowers was sitting in the shotgun seat. I grabbed for them and read the card, which said, simply, *I miss you.* No signature. A thought flashed through my brain, causing my heart to thump in my chest. *Are they from Luke?* Of course, I was immediately ashamed at the stupidity of it. They could only be from Jeremy, because only he knew the code to my car's manual lock. But somehow, having had the thought, I couldn't help but feel a little disappointed now that they weren't from Luke. Stupid, I know.

When I got back to Viewpoint, my little dilemma was still bothering me. I decided to get Agatha's opinion.

"So a friend of mine got this gift from a guy, right?" I said. "Let's say, a beautiful bouquet of flowers, for the sake of convenience. And the flowers weren't signed or anything, and this friend imagined—"

"You got flowers?" Agatha asked. "Who got you flowers?"

"I didn't say me! I said *a friend.*"

"Oh don't pull that," she said **pejoratively**. "Whenever anyone says this friend *this* and this friend *that*, they're doing a cover-up for themselves." It had taken me a while to get used to Agatha's **acerbic** wit, but I had started to really dig it. "So who're they from?" she asked.

"Jeremy," I admitted.

---

pejoratively: critically, negatively   **acerbic:** acid

"Damn! You preppy, goody-two-shoe girls get all the good stuff. The guys who like me buy me bags of incense that stink up my locker . . . So, why'd he give you flowers? I thought you two broke up."

"We did."

"Aha. Restart flowers."

"What's that?"

"Well did you *break up* break up, or like, take-a-break break up?"

"I don't know . . ."

"Is it possible that he **construed** your break up as temporary? How was it phrased?"

"Well, now that I think about it, we agreed to take a break. But it felt pretty permanent to me."

"Right. But be careful. What feels permanent to you may be a strategic ploy on his part. He may be thinking: I'll take a few weeks off, date some other girls, and then get restart flowers and go back to my safety net. When did you break up again?"

"Right before spring break," I said.

"Need I say more?"

"Hmm. Interesting."

"But what was it that you were going to say? That whole scenario about your friend getting flowers?"

"Forget it."

"Can't do it. Too late. You've brought it up, so now you'll have to follow through, or face the wrath of Agatha and be **mercilessly** throttled within inches of your life."

"Sheesh."

"Sorry. That's just the way it goes."

"I was just gonna say that when I first saw the flowers, for like a split second, I kinda sorta hoped that they were from someone else."

"Oh," she said. "Who?"

"I'd rather not tell. But is that a *bad* thing?"

---

construed: interpreted

mercilessly: cruelly, without mercy

"As far as your boyfriend goes, I'd say yeah. It's bad. Restart flowers are like jumper cables. If you get them, and you don't instantly know that that's what you've been waiting for, then it's pretty much over. Were you pining for him over break?"

"**Moderately**," I said. "Not *too* much."

"Yeah. Time to suck it up and break up for good."

"But they're such gorgeous flowers."

"If you let it drag on, he'll hate you for life."

"Yeah. You're probably right. But what about, you know, the other guy?"

"You mean Luke?" she asked.

I just smiled.

"Well, if you're wishing that the flowers were from him, then yes, that is significant."

"How significant?" I asked.

"Quite," she said. "And now, if you'll excuse me, the gentleman behind you would like to purchase a book."

moderately: not excessively; a reasonable amount

April 11: Easter

Not a big Easter turnout this year. Just my parents, myself and—as a substitute for Rico, who's off at tennis camp—my Uncle Randy. **Tremulous** about the potential of a repeat performance from Thanksgiving, Dad emptied the liquor cabinet. Mom hid her nice blown-glass vases in the basement. Personally, I was kind of looking forward to his **picaresque** stories.

But Uncle Randy was short on histrionics this time. On the contrary, he was sober, **docile**, and oddly sincere. After a casual breakfast of sausage, eggs, and toast, we went to church. Church was always nice on the holidays—everyone dressed well, and it **allayed** your fears, for an hour or so, that you might be a bad person. When we came back home, I changed into shorts and went out to shoot hoops in the driveway. After a while, Uncle Randy walked out, duck-footed and slack-jawed, still wearing his light blue polyester suit.

"Mind if I shoot a couple?" he asked.

"Of course not." I gave him a bounce pass. He dribbled a few times, his elbow bend constrained by the suit jacket. He tossed up some wacky leap-frog of a shot that went backboard, rim, backboard, and in.

"Nice shot," I said, giving him a chest pass this time. He dribbled, his eyes **fixated** on the ball and his whole body bouncing up and down in rhythm with it, like a kid who just realized he was a kid.

"You seem like you're doing all right, Uncle Randy," I said.

"You're right there," he said, giving me a little giggle.

"Uncle Randy," I said.

tremulous: shaky	**docile:** obedient	**fixated:** stuck
picaresque: roguish	**allayed:** calmed	

"Yeah?" He stopped dribbling to look at me.

"I was just wondering. I think about older people sometimes, like Mom and Dad, and I just wondered . . . do you regret anything about your life?"

He smiled, bounced the ball once with both hands, then caught it and held onto it. "Well, you know, when you're young, you worry that you'll grow up and regret not having made the right career choice, or having not traveled enough, you know, missing out on things. But I think when it comes down to it, the main regrets involve the people in your life. Your relationships."

"Oh, yeah?" I said.

"Yeah. Looking back, I wish I had told my first wife that I'd follow her to the ends of the earth. I should've covered her bed in rose petals each night. And my second wife . . . I should have told her she was a miserable witch the night I met her, because I *knew*." Randy laughed. He bounced the ball and put it in shooting position. "So, I guess that's the thing. The people that you really care about, don't be afraid to shower them with love. And the ones you don't, get out of there as quick as you can."

"Because life's short," I said.

Uncle Randy took a shot that clanged off the rim and landed in my hands. "Exactly," he said.

April 17

I sought out Jeremy today, after school, and found him at Olympia, this joint right near school where they sell candy and doughnuts and other such nutritious lures. It's the main **nexus** spot for meeting up with friends, primarily because of its **proximity** to school, but also because of the **congenial** Greek family that runs it. (What is it with me and the Greeks lately, anyway?)

When I walked in, Jeremy was sitting at a corner booth with his regular group of jock stooges. His right arm was around the shoulders of some **nondescript** sophomore blonde. Not that I cared, but it just helped seal the decision that I'd already made.

"Jeremy," I said. "I need to talk to you."

As soon as he saw me, he dropped his arm from the girl, his face going white. "Francesca, hey—"

"Outside, if you don't mind." I didn't wait for his answer. I just walked out.

I crossed my arms, enjoying the sunlight on my face. The door opened. Jeremy **affected** a casual stroll as he walked toward me. "You liked the flowers, baby?" he asked.

"I did. I wanted to thank you. They're very beautiful." I leaned in and gave him a kiss on the cheek.

"No problem," he said. "That's just my way of saying no hard feelings."

"Very effective," I said.

"To be honest," he said. "I think I'm just about ready to take you back."

---

nexus: connection, link	**congenial:** friendly	**affected:** artificially
proximity: closeness	**nondescript:** ordinary	assumed

I tried not to laugh. "Sorry, Jeremy. But I don't think that's going to work."

"*What?*"

"I appreciate the flowers, but I still think we should take a **hiatus**."

"A whuh?"

"I just know I want to stay broken up . . ." I trailed off, realizing this sounded too much like an **affront**, which I knew would translate, in Jeremy's eyes, to fighting words. "Don't be mad, please."

His lips were pulled so tight they were turning blue. "You mean *permanently?*"

"Well . . . yeah."

"Wow. That's almost funny." His tone was **caustic**. "God . . . I *made* you."

"And then you released me," I said, as **amicably** as I could manage.

"No, I didn't," he **adamantly** insisted.

"Actually, you *did*." I hadn't expected him to be this reluctant to **abdicate** his position. I crossed my arms in front of me to show I could be just as **obdurate** as him.

He snorted. "I'll bet Luke is psyched to know you're finally free for the taking."

I sighed. "Luke has no idea, Jeremy, so please don't **vilify** him. This has nothing to do with him."

"Right. I'll bet." Jeremy pressed his lips together and nodded in sarcastic **abjuration**. "Well, you two have fun together. Feel free to give him a few flowers from that bouquet I bought you."

"Come on, Jeremy," I said softly, in a last-ditch effort to **placate** him. "This really isn't about him. I just feel like our relationship has run its course, and it's time for us both to be **unfettered** for a bit. Can't we try to be nice here?"

"Cool, cool. I know a few girls who will be happy to know that

hiatus: break	**adamantly:** stubbornly	**abjuration:** retraction
affront: insult	**abdicate:** give up	**placate:** pacify
caustic: biting	**obdurate:** inflexible	**unfettered:** free
amicably: peaceably	**vilify:** slander	

I'm back on the market. I won't have any trouble finding a replacement for you, you know."

My jaw tightened. This was the last thing I wanted— **incendiary** words tossed back and forth like Chinese throwing stars. I refused to stoop to that. "That's your **prerogative**. Whatever it takes to move on. I don't understand why you're being so **sophomoric** about this, Jeremy. I was thinking we would be friends."

"Or enemies," he said. "Either way works for me."

You **impudent** *little infant.* He was pulling out all the stops to get me to **retaliate**. I pressed my tongue against the back of my teeth to keep from snapping.

"Actually, this is good," Jeremy said. "This works well. At least I know my next girl won't **torment** me until I'm blue in the face—my next girlfriend won't be afraid to have sex."

Okay, he wanted it to be like that. Well, there wasn't much I could do then.

"Bye, Jeremy," I said. I turned and walked away.

incendiary: combustible, explosive
prerogative: privilege
sophomoric: immature
impudent: disrespectful
retaliate: get even
torment: torture

April 29

Down to the wire—two weeks to go until the prom—and I'm still **deficient** in the date category. Luke and I do that thing in the hall at school, where I'm sort of looking at him, and I think he's looking at me too, but whenever the other one notices we just glance away and it never really evolves into an actual conversation. So, I'm pretty sure I was right about things being over there, even now that Jeremy and I are done and Nikki's given me the green light. Ha. Life cracks me up.

Anyway, I was walking to class between first and second periods today, and I felt a presence hovering to my left. I glanced over, and there was Eric Crowther.

"Oh," he said in that drier-than-dust **laconic** way of his. "Hey, there."

"Hi, Eric," I said.

"Yeah, so I was actually thinking of going to see a Pacers game, but they're playing like a bunch of wusses . . . and then I thought it might be fun to just sit at home and watch bad TV, just pretend it didn't exist. But I figured the only way I'd go is if you went with me . . . do you already have a prom date?"

"I—um, what?"

"Do you wanna go to the prom with me?"

It wasn't exactly the Casanova approach, but then, it was the only approach I'd gotten.

"I've got a cool tux," Eric added. "And my dad's got a Lincoln Town Car that could almost double as a limo."

---

deficient: lacking   **laconic:** brief, concise

"Sure," I said.

"What?" Eric looked all **discombobulated**.

"I said sure. I'd be happy to."

"Oh. Cool." His face lit up. "I'll pick you up at eight."

"Sounds good," I said.

"Actually, I don't know when I'll pick you up. I don't even know when the prom starts. I just wanted to say something definitive, you know . . ."

I had never heard Eric this **garrulous**. It was kind of cute. "Just call me," I said. "Whenever."

"Sure. Right." He looked around suspiciously, as though some **nefarious** hobgoblin were about to come and snatch this moment away. "I guess I'll see you then. Bye." He turned to walk away.

"Hey, Eric," I said.

"Yeah?"

"Do you want my number?"

"Oh, yeah," he said. "I'll need that."

---

discombobulated: confused **garrulous:** talkative   **nefarious:** vicious

Today the candidates for Junior Prom King and Queen were announced. Among the candidates were Jeremy, Luke, Nikki, and yours truly. I was psyched, especially since various rumors are still **circulating** about me since my big breakup with Jeremy. But then, I guess I should consider it an honor that I'm being talked about at all, considering the wallflower **anonymity** status I've held for so long. Wouldn't it be funny if Luke and I won?

Ack—I have to stop thinking about Luke!

circulating: spreading

anonymity: state of being unknown

May 17

Eric and his Lincoln Town Car showed up with remarkable **alacrity** at seven on the dot. Not unsurprisingly, his idea of a "cool tux" didn't necessarily **corroborate** the image I'd had in my head. In fact, it wasn't so much a tux as . . . not a tux. It was, in fact, according to him, a "vintage lemon yellow zoot suit." Its **abundant** accoutrement included a top hat with a feather, baggie pants tucked into black boots, and a long chain that hung from his waist to below his knees. My mom's reaction gave voice to what I was thinking: "You've got to be kidding me."

But somehow Eric pulled it off. At first, I was a little embarrassed, then ashamed that I was embarrassed, and finally not embarrassed at all, but kind of proud. The fact was, Eric was capable of something I find very difficult—flying in the face of public opinion. It turns out that what you're worried about when you imagine others are censuring the way you look is actually no big deal. For every person pointing and laughing snidely, three people would walk up and say that it was the most interesting outfit they'd ever seen.

When we pulled out of my driveway, I asked Eric where he'd made reservations. "Reservations?" he asked. Turned out he had no clue dinner was part of the night. We laughed so hard we had to pull the Town Car off the road. After a brief discussion, we decided on Texas Roadhouse, this casual steak joint with a floor covered in peanut shells. Eric said this was called "embracing the absurdity of the situation."

Our appearance at Texas Roadhouse was the closest I've ever

alacrity: promptness   **corroborate:** agree with   **abundant:** plentiful

197

been to celebrity-hood. The entire restaurant clapped for us as we paraded down the peanut-shell-littered aisle toward our corner booth, with me holding my dress up and doing little curtsies.

Eric interlocked his arm with mine and smiled at me. "Your dress," he said. "It goes so well with the peanut shells."

"And your zoot suit," I replied. "It goes so well with . . . nothing."

We laughed, sitting in a corner booth. Eric threw a peanut at me.

"You ever see the movie *Pretty in Pink*?" I asked. "Because you remind me—"

"Please don't tell me I remind you of 'Ducky Dale.' The guy who wears funny clothes and gets dissed at the prom."

Oops. I swallowed hard. For someone who would be widely considered smart, I said some pretty **asinine** things.

"I mean it's no big deal," Eric added. "I guess I just have some insecurities about being a lovable clown who no one can take seriously."

I leaned forward and blanketed Eric's hand with mine. This got his attention. I was looking him in the eye. "I wasn't trying to **intimate** that you were a Ducky, okay? You *are* lovable, but that's not such a bad thing. And I, for one, take you very seriously. I actually envy you, because you're a total **anomaly**, especially in high school. You are a true individual whose personality isn't **malleable** based on what others expect of you. You're *real*, you know, and different, and you're not afraid to **flout** the norm. Which means you're stronger than most of us. But I imagine that at times it makes you vulnerable too. But just hold tight, because when high school's over, college comes. And from what I understand, college does a better job of recognizing the genius of people like you."

"Wow." Eric's eyes were wide and a little watery. "Thanks. That's the highest **acclaim** I've ever gotten from a girl. Ever."

---

asinine: foolish
intimate: suggest

anomaly: rare event or occurrence
malleable: moldable

flout: defy
acclaim: praise

The Prom

By the time we arrived, I wondered whether I wasn't too bloated to dance. But Eric wasn't having it. He pulled me out on the floor and just started boogying. After a few dances, he decided go by the **alias** "Lothar, King of a Thousand Dances."

"Can you do the Spinning Pickle?" he asked, spinning himself on one foot until he was so nauseated he had to stop.

"And how about the Injured Duck?" He flapped his elbows up and down, one **spasmodically** and the other limply, making freaky quack noises.

The charade went on like that, until we were both sweating **profusely**. I asked Eric if he wanted a beverage and then ambled over toward the concession area. It was there, while reaching for a cup of seltzer—that I heard the lyrical **cadence** of Lucas Barton's deep, **sonorous** voice.

"See, I thought I was supposed to come alone, and then you would come alone, and by the very nature of our mutual aloneness, we would find each other and become de facto prom dates."

It was the first time he'd spoken to me in I don't know how long. Every nerve ending in my system started firing little white-hot spurts.

"That's not the way it works," I said, keeping my back to him. "You're supposed to ask me. And then I say yes, or no."

"Oh," Luke said. "See, no one ever taught me the rules."

I turned, slowly, to face him. "About what I said," I started. "At the coffeehouse that night—"

---

alias: assumed name
spasmodically: fitfully

profusely: liberally
cadence: rhythm

sonorous: loud, deep, or rich in sound

"It's okay," he cut in. "I'm sorry too."

I nodded. "So, then . . ."

Luke tapped his fingertips together. "I guess I should probably leave now, since, you know, we're not allowed to talk in public."

I rolled my eyes, then smiled. A little. "Ha ha," I said sarcastically.

Why did he have to look so amazing? Not to take anything away from Eric's zoot suit, but Luke was on a different level in his black tux, with cummerbund and bow tie, the whole deal. He had morphed from grungy X-Games to **comely** diplomat.

"So if the restraining order's up," he said, "then how come we didn't come to this thing together?"

"What?" I blurted out. What was I supposed to make of that? "Maybe because you didn't *ask* me," I said, and on cue, my muscles betrayed me, because I jerked a little and spilled some seltzer on my dress.

"Hold on," Luke said. "Stay right there." He grabbed a handful of napkins. "Where is it? Here?" Luke started rubbing at the wet spot right above my waistline. I sucked in my breath as my hands started to shake.

"Yeah." My skin felt like it was melting from the heat. "But, um, it's okay—it's just seltzer. You know, the stuff they use to get stains *out*."

He backed up, giving me a lopsided grin. "Oh. Right."

"I don't get it," I said, letting out my breath. "Why can't you just tell me what's really going on here, with us?"

He shrugged. "Well, we're at the prom, right? And, let's see, you just spilled on your dress . . ."

God, he could be so infuriating, always **equivocating**—giving an inch, and then taking it back the moment you felt comfortable with it. It wasn't the way I wanted it to be. It had been a while since I'd known how I felt, but I knew now. And I wanted him to know.

"It's too bad you can't be serious for once," I said. "Because I like you, Luke."

---

comely: attractive

equivocating: speaking evasively

"I like you too," he said.

"I don't think you understand." I grabbed him by the wrist. "I *like* you." Luke was looking into my eyes, not saying anything. "And I think you *like* me."

Nothing.

"Luke?"

"Yeah."

"Am I wrong about that?" I asked, giving him the opportunity to **disavow** before I made a complete idiot of myself.

"No," he said. "You're not wrong. I do like you."

Somehow I still wasn't sure—if he meant the words, and *how* he meant them. I thought about Connor and the jokes we'd made about his Communications major. Luke and I talked in all these gargantuan vocabulary words, but we never seemed to actually *communicate* successfully.

Before I could say anything else, Principal Adams's **stentorian** voice suddenly filled the auditorium. "Columbus High juniors, it's time to reveal your prom king and queen."

The announcement reminded me that I was actually here with a date, who I was sort of ditching at the moment. Looking over at the dance floor, I saw Eric watching me and felt a major stab of guilt.

"Look, I've gotta—"

"Go," Luke said. "We can talk later."

As I walked away from him, gliding through a sea of darkened faces and couples holding hands, I felt an odd **mixture** of relief and dread.

Eric smiled when I reached him, and he took my hand while we waited to hear whose names Principal Adams would read.

"Your prom queen this year is . . . Nicola Abrams!"

I clapped until my hands hurt, then ran up and gave her a huge hug before she made her way to the stage. I was so psyched for her. She totally deserved it—she was the most beautiful Junior Prom

---

disavow: reject   stentorian: loud   mixture: combination

Queen to ever don a tiara. And when her royal counterpart—Prom King—was announced, I'm not ashamed to admit my **gratification** that it was neither Jeremy Malone nor Luke Barton.

The rest of prom was pretty uneventful, and then the main after-prom party was out at Jack Russell's lot. I couldn't convince Eric to accompany me. He said he was too **introverted** and **misanthropic**, and he knew the party would just depress him. He gave me a kiss on the cheek, thanked me for the best night he'd had in a decade, and went off to hang with his alterna friends. I'd heard many fables of **debauchery** from parties out at Russell's lot, because it was **remote** enough that cops were less **inclined** to bust it.

I rode with Nikki and her date, Dennis. After almost a half hour of weaving along **sinuous** roads through the **arboreal** hinterland and not seeing a single car, I looked down at the map.

"This should be it right here," I said.

"Where?" Nikki said. "All I see is trees."

"I'm not sure exactly, but we just passed Youth Camp back there, so the driveway should be right here on our . . ."

Nikki jammed on the breaks so hard I thought the air bags were going to balloon out and smack her and Dennis in the face. "That's it, right?" she said.

Off to our left was an empty black hole in the trees and what appeared to be a gravel driveway. Still no cars in sight. We pulled into the driveway and followed it through a dark, tree-lined passage.

"This is total serial killer territory," Nikki said. "Maybe we should turn around."

"Just drive a little farther," Dennis said.

Soon enough, we saw traces of civilization. A few cars were parked off to the side of the road. We parked next to them and walked toward a **luminescent** orange light and the sound of music. As we grew closer, the light revealed itself as a gigantic, crackling **conflagration**.

---

gratification: satisfaction	**debauchery**: wickedness	**sinuous**: winding
introverted: withdrawn	**remote**: distant	**arboreal**: tree-filled
misanthropic: cynical	**inclined**: prone	**luminescent**: glowing
		conflagration: fire

"Yo whassup, ladies!" someone yelled at us from the porch of an **archaic** log cabin. It was Jack Russell, a senior who, before this year, was either unaware of or indifferent to my existence. "Welcome. Help yourself to whatever you want."

No other girls had arrived yet, so a **congregation** of guys encircled us, even with Dennis there. Some dude named Dave, whom I'd seen in the halls but never met, decided that we were fast friends and kept offering to refill my soda cup.

"You wanna go check out the lake?" Dave finally asked in a suspiciously **ardent** tone.

"That's okay."

"Oh come on. It's really beautiful. Check out the full moon."

I looked up and saw a big **luminous** circle looking down at us. "Yeah. It is pretty."

"Let's go check it out," Dave **cajoled**.

I felt a hand on my shoulder. "Come on, Francesca." It was Nikki. "Let's go check out the bonfire."

"Thanks for the rescue," I said as we walked away.

"No problem. The next time a guy asks you to go check out the lake with him, give me the rescue signal. Just go like this." Nikki touched her finger to her nose. It was so nice to have her back on my team.

"Got it," I said. "Thanks."

Before we could get to the fire, Nikki saw one of her dance friends. "Congratulations, Queen!" They ran toward each other and started hugging and talking. I sat on a log by the fire and stared into it, sipping my soda. I sat there, focusing on one particular ember and the way the heat seemed to pulsate through it in almost **imperceptible** wavelike motions. Fires were mesmerizing, more so than people. I'd discovered I wasn't the party type way back in eighth grade. Whenever I went to one, I tended to recoil into my own little world like this.

---

archaic: ancient	**ardent:** passionate	**cajoled:** coaxed
congregation: gathering	**luminous:** glowing	**imperceptible:** unnoticeable

"Fire's *cool*," a voice said, following it up with a Beavis-and-Butthead cackle. "Fire, fire, fire!"

I looked up. Luke was standing over me, smiling.

"Hey," I said, totally **flummoxed** by his sudden presence above me.

"You mind if I sit down?" he asked.

"Not at all."

Luke sat beside me. "Looks like you're having a pretty rockin' good time."

"Oh, shut up," I said and punched him in the shoulder. "Go get me another soda."

"Ginger ale?" he asked, with a mischievous twinkle in his eye.

"Sounds good."

He came back with a ginger ale for me, and a beer for him. "Cheers," he said.

"Cheers." We went to clink cups, but they just kind of smushed into each other.

"This is going to be my one and only beer tonight, because I'm driving," Luke said.

"Such a mature boy."

He smirked. "Yeah, too bad they can't all be like me. Francesca, I wanted to say that I'm sorry about, you know, the way the whole Jeremy thing ended up."

"It's all right. We were gonna break up eventually anyway. Things happen for a reason, I guess."

"Yeah, but I mean *the way* it happened. That was pretty lame of him."

My brow furrowed. "What do you mean?" I asked. "What do you know about it?"

Luke looked trapped. His eyes darted around **deviously** for a second and then he buried his face in his cup.

"No, really," I said. "**Enlighten** me."

"No I mean . . . you know . . . I just heard."

---

flummoxed: confused   **deviously:** deceitfully   **enlighten:** tell

"What did you hear?"

"Nothing."

"Luke. I wanna know what you heard. Tell me."

"You really do?"

I nodded.

"Okay . . ." Luke exhaled. "I heard that you went to a hotel."

"And?"

"And . . . you had sex."

I felt breath force its way out my nostrils. "And?"

"And it was your first time."

"Is that it?"

"And then he broke up with you."

"*What?*"

"You asked what I heard. That's what I heard."

"Who'd you hear it from?" I asked. "A reliable source?"

"A couple of Jeremy's friends on the team. They said he told them that's what went down."

There were no thoughts, just a surge of **unmitigated** fury. My body puffed up as if I'd been infused with extra pints of blood. I must have kicked the cup as I stood up because my foot felt wet. It squeaked as I charged off. I walked up to the first stooge in sight.

"Where's Jeremy?" I asked. Judging from the way he warily stepped back, I must have looked psychotic.

"He's right over there." He pointed.

The gap between us closed quickly. *How dare you start such a* **disparaging** *rumor about me, you duplicitous sack of dung. Thought you'd* **avenge** *your bruised ego, huh? You think you got me, but you don't even see me right now. You have no idea.* My first contact was with the cup raised to his treacherous lips. I smacked it with the palm of my hand and beer splashed everywhere.

"Hey!" someone yelled. "Cool out!"

The second contact was a decisive knee to the groin. Jeremy was

---

unmitigated: absolute   **disparaging:** degrading   **avenge:** get even for too busy processing the first blow to prepare for the second one. I doubt he saw much of anything, as he lay there crumpled up on the ground, moaning. "What the hell's wrong with you?" he cried out.

"Nothing," I said. "Feeling much better now."

"What did you do that for?"

"It's what you get for lying."

"What?" Jeremy squeaked.

"Attention, everyone!" I yelled out. "Let the record show that I never had sex with this guy!" I pointed at Jeremy.

"Oooohhh . . ."

I started to walk away, wiping the beer off on my jeans, which I'd changed into after the prom. I could feel that everyone was watching me.

"Lying? Lying! LYING!"

I turned around. Jeremy was on his feet, rushing toward me.

"You're talking to me about lying when you've been hooking up with—" He pointed at Luke, who was standing just a few feet away. "—*him*—the whole time we were going out together."

"You're crazy," I said. "That never happened."

"Oh, please! You're so full of it, both of you. You planned this whole thing to make me look like the bad guy. But I know the truth! Everyone knows the truth!"

"You wouldn't know the truth if it was **affixed** to your **epidermis**," Luke said.

Red blotches appeared on Jeremy's cheeks, and he ran right up to Luke and got in his face. "You think you're cute? You always got a line for everything. Got one lined up for when I pop you in the nose, chief?"

People were gathering around to see the **fracas**. Jeremy's eyes practically had sparks shooting out of them, but Luke's expression was **unperturbed**.

"Come on, Jeremy," I said. "Relax."

---

affixed: attached   **epidermis:** skin   **fracas:** brawl
unperturbed: composed

"No! I've been relaxed for too damn long. That's what got us into this mess. I should have clocked this guy three months ago. Then we wouldn't be having this problem."

"We'd have different problems," Luke said, maintaining his **unflinching** gaze.

"Well, you've got a problem now." Jeremy rocked back and forth, his nostrils flared.

"Don't do this, Jeremy," I begged.

He didn't even hear me. He stepped back and put up his fists. "Come on," he said to Luke. "Let's go. Let's see if you throw down as well as you ride your little board."

Luke just stood there, hands at his side.

"Come on! Let's go! You scared, man?"

"No," Luke said.

"Then come on!"

"I'm not going to fight," Luke said.

"That may not be up to you," Jeremy said.

"Yeah!" someone yelled. "Fight him, Luke!"

"I don't fight," Luke said.

"You will once I hit you," Jeremy said.

"No, actually, I won't. Your fist will collide with my face, and it will probably jerk back. Blood may even spurt. Then you'll yell 'Come on!' a few more times, until you realize I wasn't kidding, that I really *don't* fight. Then you'll walk off high five-ing your boys like a hero."

"Whatever," Jeremy said. "That's the long way of saying, 'I'm a big wuss.'"

Jeremy suddenly pulled back and swung at Luke. He stopped right before he reached his face. Luke squinted and flinched. Jeremy tapped him twice on the shoulder with his fist. "Two for flinching," Jeremy said. Then he turned to me. "Good luck with your new man. Hope you don't ever need him to protect you . . ." He walked off.

---

unflinching: relentless

"Come on, Luke!" someone yelled. "Go after him!"

People laughed, but the crowd started to **disperse** when they realized there wasn't going to be any action. I rushed right up to Luke. "I'm so sorry," I said. "Are you okay?"

"Of course I'm okay," he said, obviously **peeved**. "He didn't even touch me."

"Sorry you had to deal with that," I said.

"Yeah, so am I. You actually dated that jerk? What were you thinking?"

I pulled back, stung. Jeremy had made a huge idiot of himself, no question, and I was still furious at the stupid rumor he'd spread about us. But the thing was—Jeremy wasn't so off base to be suspicious about me and Luke. And I knew I hadn't always treated him the greatest. I'd stayed with him way past when I first had doubts about our relationship, which wasn't totally fair.

But regardless of all that, it was the same old Luke to judge me like that. Since when did I need to justify myself to him?

"I think the real question," I said, hardening my voice, "is why you get to say anything about whom I date."

I held his gaze, daring him to answer, to finally come out and say it if he really cared about me the way I cared about him.

And for a second, I thought he was going to do it—to grab me and kiss me and get all of this ridiculous will-we-or-won't-we over with once and for all.

Then his eyes glazed over, and he looked down at the ground. "Whatever," he said.

I stood there, blinking rapidly to keep from crying. My mouth filled with an acid taste, which somehow stayed after I swallowed. I looked around and saw, of all people, Agatha Renshaw alone a few feet away.

"You okay?" she asked.

"Agatha," I said. "Will you take me home?"

---

disperse: scatter   **peeved:** annoyed

May 18:
Administrative
Professionals Day

I woke up this morning with a headache the size of Rhode Island. Let's just say there was a lot of crying last night. After three Excedrin and a long hot shower, I moaned all the way downstairs.

"You don't look so good," Mom said when I walked into the kitchen.

"Don't feel so good either."

"Want a Yoo-hoo?"

I felt like I was about to cry all over again. If she knew I needed Yoo-hoo, then I must have looked bad.

I sank down at the table while she got me a nice cold Yoo-hoo out of the fridge. After a few sips, the phone rang, and I reached over to pick up.

"Hello?"

"Fran, what happened to you last night?"

"Nikki, I'm sorry. It's just, there was this huge scene with Jeremy and Luke, and then Luke and I . . ." I didn't even know how to describe it. "It just sucked, basically, so Agatha Renshaw was there, and she drove me home."

"Wait, something happened with you and Luke? I guess that's why, well, you know."

I scrunched my face up. "Why what?"

"You haven't heard?"

"Nikki, will you just tell me what's going on?"

She sighed, and I could picture her leaning against her headboard, all set to start the story. The possibilities raced through my mind, but the one I couldn't escape was the one that hurt the most. Luke had hooked up with someone else. I knew he had.

"Luke is in major trouble, Fran. Major."

I looked over at my mom, who cocked her head back at me when she saw my expression.

"He was a wreck after you took off last night—in a seriously black mood," Nikki went on. "He saw me and told me you left, but he wouldn't explain why or anything. Then he left the party, and we all thought he went home. But this morning, I heard from Shannon that Luke was caught on school grounds later on, drinking. Do you know what that means? It's grounds for *expulsion*."

"Why would he do something so stupid?" I breathed.

"Hello? Obviously whatever happened with you," she said. "You really messed him up, Fran. Now do you *finally* believe me that the jerk is completely in love with you?"

I went to see Luke today, at his house. He looked like a textbook **derelict**, with two-day stubble and that depressed, hopeless glint in his eyes. And he didn't smell too good, either. I told him to shower and shave, and then we'd talk. When he came back fifteen minutes later, he looked like a new man, but his attitude hadn't changed at all.

"Come by to take a last look at the condemned man?" he asked.

I narrowed my eyes at him. "What were you thinking?" I demanded. "Getting drunk at *school*? Come on."

"I know, I know, it was a bad move," Luke admitted. "I went there after the party, to be alone. And I thought I was showing some decent responsibility, waiting to get wasted until I was walking distance from home so I didn't have to drive anywhere."

I pursed my lips. "So you walked to the school?" I asked.

"Yeah, yeah, of course. What do you think, I'm one of those idiots who'd actually get behind the wheel loaded?"

"No, I guess you're a whole different kind of idiot," I said, starting to smile. He tossed a pillow at me. "Hey!" I objected. "I'm here to help. So wait, you went to the school to be alone . . ."

"Yeah. I needed to think." He focused his gaze on mine, and I shifted, feeling that swirly sensation inside of me that I got whenever he looked at me lately. "About what happened, at the party . . ." he began.

"It's okay," I said. "That's not important right now." I paused, thinking how a big part of this was my fault—for storming away from that party, and Luke, without giving him more of a chance.

derelict: bum

I knew he wasn't good in those moments, yet still I'd pushed him instead of just laying everything out on the table and letting him do the same. "We've got to figure out what you're gonna do."

"There's nothing I _can_ do. I'm totally, thoroughly, **irrevocably** screwed. I already had the special meeting with Principal Adams. They're kicking me out of school, which means I won't be going to college anytime soon. Unless it's like Far Eastern Nebraska State Tech Vocational College or something."

"I've heard they've got a great Forestry program," I quipped.

Luke rolled his eyes.

"Not funny," I said. "But honestly, I don't think you're gonna get kicked out of school. Not if I can help it."

"Oh, yeah. And what exactly can you do?"

"Did you forget already? It so happens that I am a founding member of the Student Disciplinary Committee."

"Ha." For the first time since I'd been there, Luke cracked a smile. "That's a good one. No, really."

"What? This is exactly this type of situation that I created the SDC for—so we'd have a **forum** to **foster** discussion between students and school officials, to challenge the **hegemony** of people like Dr. Adams. It will be a good opportunity to test the concept in its **inchoate** state."

"Suh-weet. Can't wait to be the testing ground for your failed school government bureau."

"Don't be so cynical. I'm a staunch **libertarian**, and, in my **unbiased** opinion, you were not in violation of any school codes."

"Except being drunk on school grounds," Luke said.

"Can they prove that? Tell me exactly how it all happened."

Luke leaned back, tilting his chair off the floor. "I was out at Pond Field, behind the gym, and I was having some beers. I didn't think anyone would be there, obviously. But I guess some of the cleaning crew gets there before dawn to get started, and they caught

---

irrevocably: unchangeably   **hegemony:** power   **libertarian:** individual rights
forum: meeting   **inchoate:** formless   advocate
foster: promote   **unbiased:** fair

me. Saw me drinking, the whole thing. There's not really a way out of it."

"I don't know about that."

"Listen, I appreciate your enthusiasm, but you're totally delusional. I don't have a snowball's shot in Hades, and I've already **inured** myself to that rather **noxious** fact."

"Well, at the very least, maybe I can get them to be **lenient** with you."

"Look, face it Fran, there's no chance here. Adams showed me the line in the faculty handbook—no alcohol on school premises, ever. They have every right to expel me. Now can we talk about something else, please? Hey, the SATs are a week away. Do you think you're ready?"

"I guess so. Ready as I'll ever be."

"Well, I have one last pointer for you. You should wake up early the day of the test and go running. It gets all the blood flowing to your brain."

"Really?"

"Totally," Luke said. "Trust me."

"No," I said. "Trust *me*."

---

inured: accustomed   noxious: toxic   lenient: merciful

May 23:
SAT Testing Day

I convinced Nikki to wake up early and go running with me before the test. I was totally exhausted when the alarm went off, but I did it anyway. And at first, during the test, it *did* seem to help. My mind was totally alert, and on the first three sections I finished with time to spare. But after that I started to get groggy, and my performance **waned** considerably. If I were the paranoid type, I'd have to wonder whether Luke just said that to **hamper** my test-taking ability and lower my score. But I guess we'll just have to wait and see.

waned: declined   **hamper:** obstruct

Today, for the first time in the history of Columbus High, the Student Disciplinary Committee got its day in court. I was so proud. I had advised Luke to give as few details as possible but to show how deeply he regretted his actions—which were admittedly wrong, wrong, wrong. Then he left the room, and it was time for the committee to negotiate with the administration.

Dr. Adams stood up first and, like the **disreputable despot** that he is, made his (totally biased) case against Luke. His claim was, plain and simple, that the charter of the Bartholomew County School Corporation stipulates that being caught either in possession of an open alcoholic beverage or intoxicated on school property is grounds for immediate dismissal. And from the sworn testimony of the member of the cleaning crew, Mr. Jameson, there was **incontrovertible** evidence of possession and **inebriation**.

That's when I stepped up to the plate, eager to share the ace I had up my sleeve.

"First of all, let me say that I don't think anyone on the committee here condones the behavior of Luke Barton. We agree that underage drinking, which is, of course, illegal, should also be forbidden on school property. What Luke did was stupid and reckless—although, as he pointed out, it should be considered that he did *not* intend to drive while under the influence."

"A fact which cannot be proven either way," Dr. Adams interjected.

"Granted," I said. *Ha! I just said "granted."* I felt like such an adult. "But isn't it also difficult to prove that Luke was even drunk?

---

disreputable: having a bad reputation
despot: tyrant

incontrovertible: unquestionable

inebriation: drunkenness

Mr. Jameson never called the police. He just reported what he saw directly to you. So there was never a test performed to ascertain the amount of alcohol in Luke's system, if any."

There was a low murmur in the room, and Dr. Adams actually started to look concerned. Wow, had I won this thing already?

"We understand that Mr. Barton is not subject to legal action," Dr. Adams said. "But that does not mean we cannot undertake our own action here at Columbus High. We have a rule that anyone caught with alcohol on school property will be expelled, and we are taking Mr. Jameson's report very seriously."

Okay, just as well things hadn't ended there. Because now I got to deliver my final **oratorical flourish**. "Can you show me that rule, Dr. Adams?" I asked, smiling innocently at him. "I'd like to see you point it out, in front of everyone present."

"Certainly, Ms. Castarelli." Dr. Adams reached over to the desk behind him, rifled through some papers and pulled out the county's staff handbook. He flipped through, then stopped at a page in the middle and held it up. "As you can see right here, the school system expressly prohibits drugs and alcohol on school property, with a punishment of expulsion."

"Hmm, interesting," I said. "And who has access to that handbook, Dr. Adams? Do students?"

He frowned, looking more confused than upset. He still hadn't gotten it. "No, they don't," he said. "But the students have their own handbook from which to **glean** the rules."

"Right, I'm getting to that," I said. I whipped a copy of the student handbook out of my backpack, which was lying on the desk next to me. "Exhibit A for the defense," I announced.

"Francesca, this is not a trial."

I blushed. I'd just been so excited to say that, like they did on *Law and Order*. "Feel free to read through here," I told Dr. Adams. "Every sentence, every page. And you'll see that there's nothing in

---

oratorical: theatrical   **flourish:** grand gesture   **glean:** gather

here about the policy on alcohol on school grounds. Sure, we know it's wrong, and stupid. But we, as students, would have no way of knowing that it's cause for automatic dismissal."

"Ignorance of the law—"

"Is no defense, I know. But it *is* when there's no reasonable way for us to know the law, don't you think? How can we be expected to follow a rule we aren't even allowed to read?"

Silence. Thick silence. I'd nailed them with the **linchpin**. A little research goes a long way. I'd had the idea after Luke made a reference to Dr. Adams showing him the rule in the faculty handbook. It had occurred to me that it was strange that he wouldn't have showed him the passage in the student handbook, the one we all read and had to sign a form saying we accepted at the beginning of the year.

There were a few moments of discussion, but my points were too strong. Luke was called back in, where he was informed that he would receive a brief suspension and no expulsion. Meanwhile, we all agreed that the student handbook was to be immediately revised to incorporate the rules about drugs and alcohol, because, yes, this wasn't something that should happen at Columbus High.

I just couldn't believe I'd done it—I'd saved Luke!

As I walked proudly out of the school, I was almost flattened by my **jubilant** client, Luke, who ran up and practically attacked me.

"How'd you do that?" he asked. "What did you say in there? Man, you really saved my butt."

"Oh, so *now* you believe in the Student Disciplinary Committee?"

"I do," Luke said, looking appropriately humbled for once. "And I apologize for **lampooning** your campaign."

"It's okay."

"Oh, and Francesca . . ."

"Yeah?"

"There's something I've wanted to say. For a while."

My heart started to beat faster, but I kept calm. After everything

---

linchpin: key element   **jubilant:** joyful   **lampooning:** ridiculing

Luke and I had been through this year, I wasn't about to let this be easy for him.

"What's that?"

"Well, I've been thinking . . . and, maybe you and I should, you know."

"No, I don't know," I said.

Luke groaned. "I was thinking maybe we could, like, go out or something," he mumbled.

"You were thinking *maybe*? What makes you so sure *I* want to go out with *you*, anyway?"

"Valid point," Luke said. "Hey, I've got an idea. We should get our SAT scores back in a few days. How about, whoever gets the higher score on the writing section gets to choose our fate?"

I laughed. "Like a roll of the dice?" I said. "Okay. It's a deal."

Today, directly after school, I drove to Donner Park for my meeting with Luke. The venue, the Donner Outdoor Auditorium, was picked by him for reasons he refused to explain. But it was a great choice, because today was a real **halcyon** day: bright yellow sun and a delicate breeze that tickled the leaves, the birds adding to the soft chorus with chirps and flutters. I was sitting on a bench, gazing out at the trees and ambling people, enjoying a moment of being alive, when I saw him approaching. He held a torn envelope in his right hand. Mine was in my pocket.

"Nice day, huh?" Luke took a seat at the far end of the bench.

"Absolutely beautiful," I said.

"Well, I guess the time has come, the day of our reckoning, the roll of the dice, as you so **aptly** described it."

"I guess so," I said. "You wanna go first?"

"Why don't you."

"No," I insisted. "Go ahead."

"All right." Luke slapped the envelope on the bench in front of us and smiled. "Drum roll please. . . . On the writing section of this year's SAT, Lucas William Barton is **ambivalent** to admit that his rather unimpressive score was . . . six hundred and fifty."

"YES!" I jumped up off the bench with a rebel yell. "I win! I win! You lose! I win! Ha!"

"I knew it," Luke said dejectedly. "Why, what did you get?"

"Seven hundred and twentay, baybayyyyyyyy!" I did a few more victory jumps and a spastic jog around the bench, my joy so extreme

---

halcyon: idyllic   aptly: suitably   ambivalent: of two minds

and **ineffable** that it overrode all other sensations and became the very **essence** of Francesca Castarelli at that moment.

"Oh, wait a second," Luke said. "Did I say the writing section? Because that is actually my math score."

"Shut up," I said, my joy instantly **truncated**. "What does that mean? What did you get?"

"Well, on the math section, as previously mentioned, I got a six hundred and fifty. But on the critical reading section I got a different score. It was a little higher."

"Oh, no." Apparently my victory dance—the one I was now acutely embarrassed by—had been a bit premature. I should have realized Luke would have done better than that. "What did you get?"

"A seven forty."

I sat down again and ran my hands through my hair. "Let me see your score sheet," I said. He handed it over, and there it was, plain as day: 740. As thoroughly vexed as I was by the stark reality of seeing that number, there was another emotion somewhere lurking inside of me, one that felt akin to **enraptured** anticipation. This was the way I'd envisioned it, and maybe the way I wanted it. I knew what—or I should say *whom*—I wanted. But I wanted Luke to choose.

"So, then," I said. "Congratulations."

"Thank you. Thank you very much."

"So . . ." I prompted.

"So, it looks like I won," Luke said, his mouth widening into a grin I knew all too well.

"Indeed," I said. "And, how, may I ask, do you intend to **exploit** your victory?"

"Exploit?" Luke asked.

"You know what I mean. Just say it, okay?"

"Actually, I'm really not sure I understand what you're getting at. I'm too busy basking in my own glory."

---

ineffable: indescribable   **truncated:** cut short   **exploit:** use
essence: core   **enraptured:** ecstatic

"Cute." If he kept this up, I would have to question whether I actually wanted what I thought I wanted.

"So **elucidate** for me again, quickly," Luke said. "What did you want to know?"

I pounded my fist against the park bench. "Come on, Luke. I want to know what it is you *want*."

"Oh," he said cheerily. "Why didn't you just say so? That's easy."

"And?" I asked.

"I want you."

They were the words I had been waiting for, the **figurative** key to the door of what was certain to be **utopia**. Luke Barton wanted me, and he was admitting it. My heart was pounding so loudly I could feel the blood rush in my ears.

"So, then," I said. "Isn't there something we should do to **commemorate** this emotional **apogee**?"

"Perhaps. I have a suggestion."

"I figured you might. Let's hear it."

"My vote is that we **osculate**."

"Osculate?" I asked. "What's that?"

"Let me show you," Luke said. He leaned over the bench toward me, cupped his hand against my cheek and, looking into my eyes, pressed his lips to mine in the sweetest, most delicious, perfect kiss I'd ever experienced.

---

elucidate: clarify   **utopia:** perfection   **apogee:** peak
figurative: symbolic   **commemorate:** honor   **osculate:** kiss

Glossary

A

abashed: *adj* embarrassed (16).
abated: *v* died down (73).
abdicate: *v* give up (190).
abhor: *v* hate or detest (2).
abject: *adj* despairing, cringing (61).
abjuration: *n* retraction (190).
abode: *n* home (24).
abridged: *adj* shortened (26).
abrogate: *v* end (111).
absolved: *v* forgiven (109).
abstemious: *adj* self-denying (65).
abstraction: *n* formless concept (6).
absurdity: *n* ridiculousness (6).
abundant: *adj* plentiful (197).
abysmal: *adj* terrible (73).
accede: *v* agree (165).
accentuate: *v* emphasize (91).
acclaim: *n* approval (198).
accommodate: *v* provide for (131).
accord: *n* agreement (127).
accordance: *n* agreement (4).
accost: *v* approach (23).
accretion: *n* increase (17).
accruement: *n* collection (104).
accurate: *adj* precise (34).
acerbic: *adj* acid (183).
acquiesced: *v* agreed (23).
acquired: *v* bought (175).
acumen: *n* intelligence (25).
acute: *adj* sharp (165).
adamantly: *adv* stubbornly (190).
adept: *adj* skilled (88).
adhered: *v* stuck to (87).
adjacent: *adj* next to (1).
admonishing: *v* cautioning (115).
adorned: *adj* decorated (87).
adroit: *adj* skillful (77).
adumbration: *n* symbol (127).
aesthetically: *adv* relating to beauty (16).
affected: *v* artificially assumed (189).
affirmative: *n* yes (73).
affixed: *v* attached (206).
affliction: *n* burden (83).
affluent: *adj* wealthy (2).

affront: *n* insult (190).
aggregations: *n* crowds (61).
aggrieved: *adj* upset (59).
akin: *adj* similar (21).
alacrity: *n* promptness (197).
alias: *n* assumed name (199).
allayed: *v* calmed (187).
allegiance: *n* loyalty (25).
alleviate: *v* lessen (157).
allocated: *v* given (131).
allotted: *adj* prearranged (38).
aloof: *adj* standoffish (1).
altruism: *n* self-sacrifice (19).
amassing: *v* collecting (24).
ambience: *n* atmosphere (140).
ambivalent: *adj* of two minds (221).
amend: *v* change (111).
amends: *n* apologies (35).
amicably: *adv* peaceably (190).
amnesty: *n* forgiveness (100).
amorous: *adj* interested in love (erotic) (173).
analogy: *n* comparison (116).
anecdote: *n* story (66).
animosity: *n* hatred (83).
anomaly: *n* rare event or occurrence (198).
anonymity: *n* state of being unknown (195).
anonymous: *adj* lacking identity (134).
anthropologist: *n* scientist of human development (52).
anticipation: *n* state of expectation (33).
anticlimactic: *adj* disappointing (43).
antipathy: *n* dislike (47).
antiquated: *adj* old (111).
antithesis: *n* exact opposite (119).
anxiety: *n* unease (51).
apathetic: *adj* uninterested (7).
apex: *n* height (15).
aplomb: *n* poise (25).
apogee: *n* peak (223).
apprehension: *n* nervousness (76).
approbation: *n* approval (81).
approximating: *v* resembled (102).
aptitude: *n* ability (73).
aptly: *adv* suitably (221).
aquatic: *adj* sea (126).

arbitration: *n* negotiation (109).
arboreal: *adj* tree-filled (202).
archaic: *adj* ancient (203).
ardent: *adj* passionate (203).
arduous: *adj* difficult (25).
arsenal: *n* weapons storehouse (177).
artfully: *adv* skillfully (127).
articulate: *adj* well-spoken (3).
artisans: *n* craftsmen (141).
ascend: *v* climb (75).
ascertained: *v* determined (90).
ascribed: *v* attributed (165).
asinine: *adj* foolish (198).
aspirations: *n* ambitions (50).
assassinated: *v* killed (23).
assemblage: *n* group (141).
assented: *v* agreed (89).
assessment: *n* evaluation (7).
assuage: *v* ease (147).
attained: *v* achieved (171).
atypical: *adj* out of character (19).
augur: *n* prediction (75).
authoritatively: *adv* with command (16).
automatons: *n* robots (103).
avail: *n* benefit (43).
avenge: *v* get even for (205).
averred: *v* affirmed (73).
avert: *v* turn aside (3).
awry: *adv* out of kilter, wrong (34).

B

ballad: *n* song (132).
balustrade: *n* railing (106).
banal: *adj* bland (1).
banter: *v* chit-chat (6); *n* conversation (51).
bashfully: *adv* shyly (24).
bated: *adj* restrained (24).
beatific: *adj* saintly (34).
befuddled: *adj* confused (45).
begrudgingly: *adv* resentfully (89).
behemoths: *n* mighty animals (171).
beneficence: *n* good will (84).
benevolent: *adj* noble (171).
benign: *adj* harmless (99).
bereft: *adj* lacking (134).
beseeched: *v* pleaded (62).
beset: *adj* troubled, harassed (25).
besieged: *v* overtaken (141).
bevy: *n* crowd (15).
bilked: *v* tricked (50).
blanched: *v* went pale (11).
blasé: *adj* unthinking (103).

blatant: *adj* obvious (22).
bliss: *n* delight (31).
boisterously: *adv* energetically (165).
bolster: *v* strengthen (26).
bombastic: *adj* pompous (26).
brash: *adj* bold (46).
bravado: *n* boldness (105).
brazen: *adj* bold (175).
breadth: *n* scope (99).
brevity: *n* briefness (105).
brusquely: *adv* abruptly (51).
bulwark: *n* wall (143).
buoyant: *adj* cheerful (165).
burgeoning: *adj* bursting (175).

C

cadence: *n* rhythm (199).
cajoled: *v* coaxed (203).
callous: *adj* unfeeling (106).
camaraderie: *n* companionship (62).
candidacy: *n* standing for office (49).
capitulated: *v* surrendered (8).
capricious: *adj* fickle (141).
captivating: *adj* appealing (141).
carousing: *adj* partying (175).
cascading: *v* pouring (23).
cataclysmic: *adj* disastrous (65).
catalog: *n* directory (37).
catalyst: *n* something that brings about a change (2).
caucuses: *n* assemblies (50).
caustic: *adj* biting (190).
cavernous: *adj* huge and empty (15).
cavorting: *v* frolicking (107).
celerity: *n* speed (140).
censuring: *v* criticizing (65).
cerebral: *adj* brainy or intelligent (3).
certitude: *n* assurance (34).
chagrined: *adj* ashamed (69).
chaos: *n* disorder (42).
charlatans: *n* frauds (143).
chastise: *v* criticize, rebuke (88).
cherub: *n* angel (16).
chortled: *v* laughed (54).
churlishness: *n* rudeness (90).
circulating: *v* spreading (195).
circumlocution: *n* roundabout speech (57).
circumnavigating: *v* going around (132).
circumscribed: *v* confined (106).
civility: *n* politeness (24).
clairvoyance: *n* perceptiveness (26).
clamor: *n* noise (132).

clandestinely: *adv* secretly (166).
cleft: *adj* cracked (171).
clique: *n* group (42).
clout: *n* power (55).
cloying: *adj* sickly sweet (42).
coalescence: *n* grouping (62).
cogitation: *n* reflection (99).
coherent: *adj* rational (44).
coincidence: *n* pure chance (21).
collective: *n* group (142).
colluding: *v* scheming (148).
colossal: *adj* huge (126).
combative: *adj* argumentative (37).
comely: *adj* attractive (200).
commemorate: *v* honor (223).
commendable: *adj* admirable (166).
compassion: *n* sympathy (126).
complemented: *v* matched (5).
compliment: *n* flattering remark (27).
comply: *v* obey (100).
composed: *v* made up of (62).
composure: *n* self-control (33).
concede: *v* grant (26).
conceited: *adj* proud (88).
concept: *n* idea (47).
conciliatory: *adj* appeasing (113).
concise: *adj* brief (37).
concurred: *v* agreed (52).
condescending: *adj* degrading (4).
confection: *n* candy (101).
confidante: *n* friend entrusted with secrets (179).
conflagration: *n* fire (202).
confounded: *adj* confused (116).
congenial: *adj* friendly (189).
congregation: *n* gathering (203).
conniving: *n* scheming (42).
consanguinity: *n* kinship (87).
conscience: *n* moral sense (23).
consequence: *n* result (149).
consoling: *v* comforting (128).
conspicuous: *adj* noticeable (12).
construed: *v* interpreted (184).
contended: *v* argued (79).
context: *n* setting (16).
conundrum: *n* puzzle or riddle (19).
convened: *v* called together (57).
conventional: *adj* normal (89).
convictions: *n* beliefs (50).
convivial: *adj* sociable (143).
copious: *adj* plentiful (41).
coquettish: *adj* flirtatious (38).
corroborate: *v* agree with (197).

coup: *n* brilliant act (107).
covert: *adj* secret (12).
covet: *v* desire (42).
coy: *adj* shy (42).
credibility: *n* trustworthiness (12).
criteria: *n* decisive factor (84).
cronies: *n* buddies (49).
crux: *n* core (116).
cupidity: *n* greed (141).
cursory: *adj* brief (112).
curtly: *adv* tersely (37).
cynical: *adj* negative (39).

D

dauntless: *adj* fearless (12).
dawdle: *v* hang around (140).
dearth: *n* lack (88).
debacle: *n* disaster (42).
debauchery: *n* wickedness (202).
decipher: *v* decode (38).
defamatory: *adj* destroying a reputation (66).
defer: *v* postpone (113).
deficient: *adj* lacking (193).
deft: *adj* skilled (81).
deified: *v* made god-like (100).
deign: *v* lower oneself (88).
dejectedly: *adv* unhappily (77).
delectable: *adj* tasty (5).
delegates: *n* representatives (131).
deleterious: *adj* harmful (100).
deliberation: *n* consideration (49).
delineating: *v* defining (106).
delirious: *adj* feverish (121).
deluding: *v* deceiving (26).
demeanor: *n* manner (37).
deplorable: *adj* terrible (22).
deprecating: *adj* insulting (174).
deranged: *adj* crazy (21).
derelict: *n* bum (211).
descending: *adj* downward (3).
desiccated: *adj* dried out (24).
despondent: *adj* depressed (179).
despot: *n* tyrant (217).
deter: *v* discourage (172).
detest: *v* strongly dislike (21).
deviously: *adv* deceitfully (204).
diatribe: *n* attack (125).
diffident: *adj* timid (169).
digress: *v* wander (109).
dilapidated: *adj* run down (65).
diligent: *adj* hard working (15).
diminished: *v* lessened (127).

diminutive: *adj* tiny (83).
din: *n* clamor or noise (12).
diplomacy: *n* skillful negotiation (12).
disarming: *adj* charming (25).
disavow: *v* reject (201).
discerns: *v* detects (83).
discipline: *n* self-control (11).
disclosure: *n* admission (47).
discombobulated: *adj* confused (194).
discomfiting: *adj* unsettling (171).
disconsolately: *adv* miserably (84).
disdainfully: *adv* scornfully (20).
disequilibrium: *n* inequality (78).
disinterest: *n* lack of concern (25).
dismissive: *adj* haughty (24).
disparaging: *adj* degrading (205).
disparate: *adj* not similar (30).
disparities: *n* differences (3).
dispassionate: *adj* indifferent (88).
disperse: *v* scatter (208).
disposition: *n* character (128).
disreputable: *adj* having a bad reputation (217).
disseminating: *v* spreading (33).
dissented: *v* disagreed (34).
dissipated: *v* dissolved (125).
dissonant: *adj* unmusical (72).
dissuade: *v* discourage (100).
distended: *adj* swollen (172).
distinguish: *v* tell between (29).
distraught: *adj* upset (15).
diverted: *v* sidetracked (62).
divulged: *v* revealed (69).
docile: *adj* obedient (187).
dolorous: *adj* mournful (126).
dominion: *n* power (41).
dotard: *n* old person (173).
doting: *adj* devoted (35).
dousing: *v* drenching (15).
dubious: *adj* doubtful (65).
dumbfounded: *adj* astonished (19).
dunce: *n* idiot (4).
duplicitous: *adj* dishonest (87).
dwindling: *adj* shrinking (46).

E

eavesdropping: *adj* snooping or listening in (29).
ebullient: *adj* high-spirited (2).
eclectic: *adj* selective (131).
ecstatic: *adj* overjoyed (6).
edicts: *n* laws (49).
edification: *n* instruction (54).
effeminate: *adj* feminine (87).

efficacious: *adj* effective (84).
effulgent: *adj* brilliant or radiant (3)
effusiveness: *n* gushiness (69).
egalitarian: *adj* democratic (50).
egomaniac: *n* self-centered person (23).
egregious: *adj* conspicuous (177).
elaborately: *adv* with great care, at length (35).
élan: *n* flair (166).
elated: *adj* overjoyed (115).
elegant: *adj* refined (88).
eloquently: *adv* expressively (91).
elucidate: *v* clarify (223).
elusive: *adj* hard to pin down (20).
emaciated: *adj* very thin (6).
emanating: *v* originating (42).
emancipated: *v* liberated (175).
embellished: *v* decorated (5).
emboldened: *adj* encouraged (34).
emitting: *v* giving off (3).
empathy: *n* compassion (22).
enacting: *v* acting (100).
enclave: *n* closed society (2).
encore: *n* repeat performance (91).
enigmatic: *adj* mysterious (58).
enlighten: *v* tell (204).
enmity: *n* hostility (67).
ennui: *n* boredom (25).
enraptured: *adj* ecstatic (222).
enshrouded: *v* enclosed (134).
enthralled: *adj* enchanted (21).
entreated: *v* begged (163).
environs: *n* surroundings (37).
epicenter: *n* precise center (41).
epidemic: *n* plague (99).
epidermis: *n* skin (206).
epiphany: *n* divine realization (49).
epithet: *n* nickname (152).
epitome: *n* ideal (171).
equivocating: *v* speaking evasively (200).
erroneously: *adv* wrongly (38).
ersatz: *adj* false (59).
erudite: *adj* scholarly (17).
erupted: *v* burst forth (12).
essence: *n* core (222).
essentially: *adv* basically (17).
estranged: *v* alienated (166).
euphonious: *adj* pleasant sounding (12).
euphoric: *adj* overjoyed (69).
evince: *v* reveal (101).
exalted: *adj* glorious (116).
excerpt: *n* brief passage (35).
exclusivity: *n* selectiveness (89).

exculpated: *v* freed from blame (100).
excursion: *n* outing (106).
exemplary: *adj* excellent (84).
exhorted: *v* urged (20).
exhumed: *v* dug up (29, 109).
exoneration: *n* pardon (100).
exorbitantly: *adv* excessively (83).
expeditious: *adj* swift (51).
expiate: *v* make amends for (99).
explicitly: *adv* specifically (58).
exploit: *v* use (222).
extant: *adj* existing (171).
extensively: *adv* in-depth (24).
extenuating: *adj* outside influences (51).
extraneous: *adj* unneeded (39).
extricate: *v* remove (176).
exuberance: *n* enthusiasm (20).
exude: *v* give off (71).

F

fabricated: *adj* fictional (66).
faceted: *adj* sided (84).
fallible: *adj* imperfect (29).
fantastical: *adj* wonderful (134).
fathom: *v* understand (100).
fatigue: *n* exhaustion (33).
fealty: *n* loyalty (105).
fecund: *adj* fertile (23).
feigning: *v* faking (7).
felicitous: *adj* fortunate (83).
fervent: *adj* intense (133).
figurative: *adj* symbolic (223).
fixated: *v* stuck (187).
flagrant: *adj* obvious (46).
flanked: *v* surrounded (62).
flaunt: *v* show off (66).
flecked: *v* speckled (25).
flippantly: *adv* disrespectfully (24).
flouncing: *v* prancing (62).
flourish: *n* grand gesture (218).
flout: *v* defy (198).
flummoxed: *adj* confused (204).
flustered: *adj* upset, confused (33).
fodder: *n* food (41).
forbearance: *n* patience (171).
foreboding: *adj* ominous (105).
forego: *v* give up (51).
foreseeing: *v* predicting (12).
forlorn: *adj* sad or dejected (5).
forte: *n* strong point (6).
fortuitously: *adv* luckily (73).
forum: *n* meeting (212).

foster: *v* promote (212).
fracas: *n* brawl (206).
fraught: *adj* filled (37).
frivolous: *adj* trivial (103).
frugal: *adj* thrifty (22).
fundamental: *adj* basic (50).
furtively: *adv* secretively (147).
futile: *adj* pointless (26).

G

gaiety: *n* cheerfulness (62).
gait: *n* way of walking (2).
gamboling: *v* skipping (75).
gamut: *n* spectrum (6).
gape: *v* stare (42).
gargantuan: *adj* enormous (42).
garish: *adj* gaudy (111).
garnering: *v* gaining (42).
garrulous: *adj* talkative (194).
gaudiest: *adj* flashiest (87).
genial: *adj* friendly (24).
gingerly: *adv* carefully (102).
glean: *v* gather (218).
glitches: *n* snags (131).
glum: *adj* sad (87).
goading: *n* prodding (8).
gourmands: *n* food lovers (84).
grace: *v* honor (25).
grandiloquently: *adv* pompously (79).
gratification: *n* satisfaction (202).
gratifying: *adj* rewarding (97).
gratis: *adj* free (81).
gratitude: *n* thankfulness (72).
gregarious: *adj* outgoing (175).
grievous: *adj* serious (63).
grim: *adj* dismal (35).
grossly: *adv* hugely (25).
guise: *n* excuse (38, 140).

H

halcyon: *adj* idyllic (221).
hamper: *v* obstruct (215).
hapless: *adj* miserable (105).
haranguing: *v* criticizing (105).
harrowing: *adj* distressing (72).
haughty: *adj* proud (1).
havoc: *n* chaos (150).
hedged: *v* dodged (47).
hegemony: *n* power (212).
heretofore: *adv* until now (67).
hiatus: *n* break (190).
hierarchy: *n* chain of command (1).

histrionic: *adj* dramatic (61).
honed: *v* sharpened (73).
horde: *n* crowd (50).
hubris: *n* arrogance (53).
hypothetically: *adv* theoretically (37).

I

iconoclastic: *adj* radical (66).
idolatry: *n* worship (38).
ignoble: *adj* dishonorable (12).
ignominiously: *adv* shamefully (37).
illiterate: *adj* uneducated (22).
illuminated: *adj* lighted (88).
imbeciles: *n* idiots (42).
imbibed: *v* drank (85).
imbroglio: *n* mess (100).
immaculate: *adj* spotless (151).
immaterial: *adj* unimportant (39).
immense: *adj* huge (126).
immerse: *v* plunge (37).
immorality: *n* corruption (62).
immortal: *adj* undying (63).
immutable: *adj* unchangeable (6).
impasse: *n* standstill (29).
impassive: *adj* emotionless (77).
imperative: *adj* essential (62).
imperceptible: *adj* unnoticeable (203).
imperious: *adj* domineering (41).
impetus: *n* incentive (140).
implausible: *adj* unbelievable (140).
implicit: *adj* implied (4).
import: *n* meaning (23).
importuned: *v* pestered (151).
impromptu: *adj* last minute (57).
impudent: *adj* disrespectful (191).
inanity: *n* stupidity (62).
inaudible: *adj* too soft to hear (132).
incandescence: *n* radiance (171).
incapacitated: *adj* unable (35).
incendiary: *adj* combustible, explosive (191).
incensed: *adj* angry (58).
incentive: *n* motivation (22).
inchoate: *adj* formless (212).
incidentally: *adv* by the way (119).
incisive: *adj* perceptive (79).
inclined: *adj* prone (202).
incoherently: *adv* inarticulately (57).
incongruous: *adj* incompatible (74).
inconsolable: *adj* heart-broken (125).
incontrovertible: *adj* unquestionable (217).
incredible: *adj* extraordinary (38).
incredulous: *adj* disbelieving (119).

incrementally: *adv* increasingly (75).
incurred: *v* brought on oneself (163).
indecorous: *adj* impolite (66).
indefatigable: *adj* tireless (33).
indifferent: *adj* uncaring (61).
indigence: *n* poverty (103).
indignantly: *adv* angrily (43).
indolent: *adj* lazy (6).
industrious: *adj* hard-working (26).
inebriation: *n* drunkenness (217).
ineffable: *adj* indescribable (222).
inertia: *n* sluggishness (151).
inexplicable: *adj* unexplainable (7).
infamous: *adj* well-known (33).
infidelities: *n* disloyalties (45).
influx: *n* flood (141).
infuriated: *v* angered (27).
infusion: *n* outpouring (170).
ingenious: *adj* brilliant (46).
ingénue: *n* naïve young girl (173).
ingratiating: *adj* flattering (140).
inherently: *adv* essentially (116).
inhibit: *v* restrain (5).
inimitable: *adj* unique (51).
initiative: *n* proposal (112).
inkling: *n* suspicion (57).
innocuous: *adj* harmless (7).
inquired: *v* asked (31).
inquisitive: *adj* questioning (62).
inscrutable: *adj* unreadable (141).
insidiousness: *n* sinister nature (100).
insolent: *adj* rude (47).
instills: *v* imparts (87).
insufferable: *adj* unbearable (51).
intangibles: *n* subtleties (84).
integral: *adj* essential (52).
intentions: *n* goals (53).
interloper: *n* intruder (175).
interminable: *adj* endless (23).
interrogation: *n* questioning (37).
intimate: *v* suggest (198).
intimated: *v* hinted (88).
intimidating: *adj* frightening (34).
intrepid: *adj* fearless (12).
intricate: *adj* complex (87).
intriguing: *adj* interesting (2).
introverted: *adj* withdrawn (202).
inured: *v* accustomed (213).
invective: *n* criticism (45).
inveterate: *adj* habitual (141).
involuntarily: *adv* automatically (106).
iota: *n* bit (71).

irate: *adj* angry (23).
iridescent: *adj* shimmering (72).
ironic: *adj* contrary to appearances (79).
irrational: *adj* not logical (3).
irrevocably: *adv* unchangeably (212).

J
jettisoned: *v* abandoned (170).
jubilant: *adj* joyful (219).

K
knell: *n* chime (66).
kowtow: *v* bow down to (153).
kudos: *n* praise, applause (34).

L
laborious: *adj* difficult (49).
labyrinthine: *adj* maze-like (106).
lacerated: *v* slashed (172).
lackadaisical: *adj* lazy (65).
lackluster: *adj* unimpressive (149).
laconic: *adj* brief, concise (193).
lamenting: *v* grieving (143).
lampooning: *v* ridiculing (219).
languish: *v* suffer (151).
largesse: *n* generosity (87).
latent: *adj* hidden (29).
lauded: *v* praised (87).
legerdemain: *n* sleight of hand (21).
legion: *n* crowd (106).
legislation: *n* law (50).
lenient: *adj* merciful (213).
lethargically: *adv* lazily (43).
libertarian: *n* individual rights advocate (212).
lilting: *adj* rhythmic (143).
linchpin: *n* key element (219).
livid: *adj* furious (52).
loathed: *v* hated (41).
lofty: *adj* superior (3).
loitering: *v* loafing (140).
longevity: *n* long life (41).
looted: *adj* burgled (69).
loquacious: *adj* talkative (15).
lout: *n* thug (66).
luminescent: *adj* glowing (202).
luminous: *adj* glowing (203).
lurch: *v* pitch forward (74).
luxuriant: *adj* lush (72).

M
machinations: *n* schemes (22).

magnanimously: *adv* generously (19).
magnitude: *n* extent (99).
majestic: *adj* grand (128).
malleable: *adj* moldable (198).
mandated: *v* commanded (47).
materialized: *v* appeared (65).
maternal: *adj* motherly (15).
matriarch: *n* ruling female (24).
matriculating: *v* beginning school (174).
maudlin: *adj* sappy (8).
maxim: *n* saying (31).
melancholia: *n* depression (127).
mellifluous: *adj* smooth-sounding (24).
melodrama: *n* showy drama (101).
mendacious: *adj* dishonest (33).
mercilessly: *adv* cruelly, without mercy (184).
mercurially: *adv* unpredictably (61).
mesmerized: *adj* captivated (143).
metamorphosing: *v* changing (20).
metaphors: *n* comparisons (150).
miasma: *n* haze (62).
milieu: *n* environment (79).
mimicking: *v* imitating (30).
minute: *adj* precise (137).
minutiae: *n* details (41).
misanthropic: *adj* cynical (202).
misconduct: *n* bad behavior (63).
mixture: *n* combination (201).
mock: *adj* fake (26).
moderately: *adv* not excessively; a reasonable amount (185).
modicum: *n* little bit (79).
modulated: *v* moderated (47).
mollify: *v* subdue (29).
monotony: *n* dullness (99).
morass: *n* tangle (38).
moratorium: *n* an end (29).
morbid: *adj* gloomy (127).
moribund: *adj* dying (143).
mortal: *adj* human (39).
multitude: *n* huge number (61).
mundane: *adj* ordinary (26).
myopic: *adj* short-sighted (33).
myriad: *adj* numerous (25).

N
nadir: *n* rock bottom (99).
naïve: *adj* inexperienced (1).
naïvely: *adv* innocently (105).
nefarious: *adj* vicious (194).
negligence: *n* inattention (105).
nemesis: *n* enemy (90).

neophyte: *n* beginner (3).
nexus: *n* connection, link (189).
nonconformist: *n* rebel (67).
nondescript: *adj* ordinary (189).
nook: *n* alcove (49).
notion: *n* idea (140).
noxious: *adj* toxic (38, 213).

O

obdurate: *adj* hard-hearted, inflexible (35, 190).
obeisant: *adj* submissive (140).
obese: *adj* very overweight (6).
objective: *adj* impartial (58).
obliquely: *adv* indirectly (66).
oblivious: *adj* unaware (174).
obscured: *adj* covered (19).
obstinate: *adj* stubborn (8).
obstreperous: *adj* hostile (33).
odious: *adj* horrible (87).
ogling: *v* eyeing (39).
opportune: *adj* timely (38).
optimal: *adj* best (103).
optimism: *n* cheerfulness (19).
opulent: *adj* showy (43).
oration: *n* speech (11).
oratorical: *adj* theatrical (218).
ornately: *adv* elaborately (87).
osculate: *v* kiss (223).
ostracize: *v* exile (38).
otiose: *adj* useless (26).
overwrought: *adj* exaggerated (153).
overzealous: *adj* overly eager (89).
oxymoron: *n* contradiction (100).

P

pacified: *v* calmed (72).
palatial: *adj* palace-like (42).
paltry: *adj* limited (67).
panorama: *n* view (73).
paradoxically: *adv* in contradiction (41).
paragon: *n* ideal (38).
pariah: *n* outsider (38).
parody: *n* spoof (30).
paroxysms: *n* spasms (72).
particularly: *adv* specifically (2).
pathos: *n* pity (38).
patronage: *n* monetary support (22).
pauper: *n* poor person (103).
peccadilloes: *n* failings (83).
pedagogical: *adj* instructive (51).
peeved: *adj* annoyed (208).

pejoratively: *adv* critically, negatively (183).
penchant: *n* fondness (30).
penurious: *adj* needy (109).
peons: *n* little folks (66).
perimeter: *n* outside edge (166).
peripheral: *adj* within the outer part of the field (of vision) (144).
periphery: *n* edges (132).
perpetually: *adv* continually (83).
persevered: *v* kept trying (3).
persistence: *n* endurance (33).
pertinent: *adj* relevant (79).
peruse: *v* examine (4).
petulant: *adj* ill-tempered (79).
phenomenon: *n* fact or event (2).
picaresque: *adj* roguish (187).
pinnacle: *n* top (73).
placate: *v* pacify (190).
plagiarism: *n* copying (49).
plateau: *n* level (74).
plaudits: *n* applause (27).
plenitude: *n* abundance (169).
plethora: *n* excess (175).
pliable: *adj* bendable (19).
ploy: *n* tactic or strategy (12).
plucky: *adj* gutsy (170).
plunder: *n* booty (69).
poised: *v* composed (25).
polemics: *n* arguments (26).
pompous: *adj* pretentious, self-important (7).
pontificating: *n* preaching (49).
portly: *adj* stout (166).
poseur: *n* pretender (30).
posited: *v* put forward (117).
potables: *n* drinks (65).
prattled: *v* chatted (24).
prattling: *v* blathering (90).
precedes: *v* comes before (2).
predicament: *n* dilemma (149).
predominantly: *adv* mainly (62).
premises: *n* grounds (65).
preoccupied: *adj* lost in thought (38).
prerogative: *n* privilege (191).
presumed: *v* supposed (27).
presumptuous: *adj* assuming (53).
pretentious: *adj* pompous (74).
prevaricate: *v* lie (149).
procured: *v* obtained (103).
prodding: *n* urging (89).
prodigious: *adj* remarkable (57).
profusely: *adv* liberally (199).
prognostication: *n* prediction (54).

progressive: *adj* favoring change (50).
prominent: *adj* well-known (15).
pronounce: *v* declare (95).
proportional: *adj* relative (83).
proportionate: *adj* balanced (90).
proposition: *n* offer (81).
proscribe: *v* ban (105).
prospect: *n* possibility (47).
protocol: *n* procedure (5).
protracted: *adj* extended (65).
provincial: *adj* unsophisticated (8).
provoke: *v* incite (90).
prowess: *n* skill (26).
proximity: *n* closeness (189).
proxy: *n* substitution (22).
prudently: *adv* wisely (101).
pugnacious: *adj* aggressive (42).
punctual: *adj* on time (25).

Q

quash: *v* suppress (47).
quell: *v* soothe (97).
querulous: *adj* argumentative (29).
quivering: *v* trembling (21).
quixotic: *adj* idealistic (55).

R

raconteur: *n* story teller (66).
radiant: *adj* glowing (24).
railed: *v* ranted (19).
random: *adj* patternless (26).
rankled: *adj* irritated (51).
rant: *n* lecture (3).
rapport: *n* mutual understanding (20).
rarity: *n* uncommon circumstance (132).
rationalization: *n* reason (65).
raucous: *adj* wild (106).
realm: *n* territory (38).
rebutted: *v* argued back (66).
reciprocating: *v* returning (37).
reclusive: *adj* solitary (165).
recoil: *v* withdraw (38).
reconcile: *v* reunite, restore to friendship (177).
reconnaissance: *n* spying (53).
recriminated: *v* accused (174).
recurrent: *adj* repeat (104).
refuted: *v* denied (79).
regurgitating: *v* spitting up (57).
reiterated: *v* repeated (47).
relented: *v* yielded (155).
relishing: *v* savoring (12).
remote: *adj* distant (202).

rendezvous: *n* meeting (144).
rendition: *n* version (49).
renouncing: *v* rejecting (26).
renowned: *adj* well-known (88).
repudiates: *v* rejects (42).
rescind: *v* take back (66).
resilient: *adj* durable (172).
resolution: *n* promise (4).
resonance: *n* character or tone (4).
resplendence: *n* brilliance (132).
restive: *adj* restless (105).
restraint: *n* self-control (170).
resume: *v* begin again (81).
retaliate: *v* get even (191).
retort: *n* angry reply (52).
revel: *v* enjoy (19).
revelation: *n* realization (13).
reverberated: *v* echoed (19).
revered: *v* respected (59).
reverie: *n* musing (116).
rhapsodizing: *v* praising (105).
rhetorical: *adj* asked for effect (17).
rife: *adj* filled (19).
ritual: *n* tradition (5).
robust: *adj* healthy (71).
rollicking: *adj* high-spirited (106).
rousing: *adj* inspiring (11).
ruminated: *v* thought about (17).
ruse: *n* trick (12).

S

sabotage: *v* damage (143).
saccharine: *adj* overly sweet (19).
sagacious: *adj* wise (171).
salient: *adj* significant (3).
salutations: *n* greetings (65).
sanctioned: *v* allowed (105).
sardonically: *adv* sarcastically (55).
sartorially: *adv* style of dress (17).
satiated: *v* satisfied (105).
satires: *n* spoofs (79).
saturating: *v* soaking (126).
sauntered: *v* strolled (170).
scrutinize: *v* examine closely (16).
sedateness: *n* calm (177).
segues: *v* leads (109).
serendipity: *n* luck (19).
serene: *adj* peaceful (49).
shrewdness: *n* knowledge (71).
simultaneously: *adv* at the same time (141).
sinewy: *adj* lean (25).
sinuous: *adj* winding (202).

smirking: *v* grinning (61).
smug: *adj* self-satisfied (4).
snide: *adj* nasty (79).
sniveling: *adj* whining (81).
snubbed: *v* rejected (75).
sobriety: *n* abstinence (42).
sobriquet: *n* nickname (41).
solarium: *n* sunroom (134).
solemnly: *adv* seriously (52).
solicitously: *adv* kindly (31).
solidarity: *n* unity (34).
solipsistic: *adj* self-centered (153).
sonorous: *adj* loud, deep, or rich in sound (199).
sophomoric: *adj* immature (191).
spasmodically: *adv* fitfully (199).
spurious: *adj* false (49).
spurred: *v* prompted (42).
stagnant: *adj* stale (137).
stalemate: *n* standoff (33).
stalwart: *adj* robust (42).
stentorian: *adj* loud (201).
stifle: *v* cover (43).
stilted: *adj* stiff (29).
stimulating: *adj* exciting (58).
stoic: *adj* stone-faced (17).
stolid: *adj* indifferent (3).
stratagem: *n* scheme (105).
strictures: *n* limits (105).
strident: *adj* loud (42).
stupefied: *adj* amazed (135).
sublime: *adj* splendid (72).
submissive: *adj* obedient (52).
subsided: *v* died down (174).
substantiate: *v* validate (55).
substantive: *adj* real or solid (17).
subtle: *adj* understated (16).
succinct: *adj* brief (20).
succumbed: *v* surrendered (72).
sufficient: *adj* enough (109).
suggestively: *adv* implying indecency (62).
sullen: *adj* grim (165).
sultriest: *adj* steamiest (38).
supercilious: *adj* arrogant (125).
superfluous: *adj* unnecessary (38).
suppress: *v* stifle (24).
surmised: *v* guessed (43).
surreal: *adj* unreal or strange (13).
swarthy: *adj* of dark complexion (152).
synchronicity: *n* harmony (76).

T

taciturn: *adj* silent (73).

tactic: *n* method (58).
tantalizing: *adj* tempting (89).
tantamount: *adj* equal (26).
tardiness: *n* lateness (24).
tedious: *adj* dull or tiresome (6).
temerity: *n* boldness (106).
tenaciously: *adv* stubbornly (7).
tenet: *n* theory (50).
tenuous: *adj* shaky (155).
terrestrial: *adj* earthly (172).
threshold: *n* entrance (69).
tidings: *n* news (55).
timorously: *adv* bashfully (69).
tirade: *n* outburst (45).
toiling: *v* working (131).
torment: *v* torture (191).
tranquil: *adj* calm (99).
transcendent: *adj* awe-inspiring (72).
transfixed: *adj* spellbound (9).
transgression: *n* misbehavior (106).
transient: *adj* brief (176).
transpired: *v* happened (165).
tremulous: *adj* shaky (187).
trifle: *n* little thing (42).
trite: *adj* stale, commonplace (166).
triumphant: *adj* victorious (91).
triumvirate: *n* threesome (41).
troupe: *n* group (33).
trumped: *v* talked up (89).
truncated: *v* cut short (222).
turgid: *adj* swollen (71).

U

ubiquitous: *adj* everywhere (65).
ulterior: *adj* hidden (117).
unabashed: *adj* unashamed (2).
unassumingly: *adv* modestly (25).
unbiased: *adj* fair (212).
unbridled: *adj* unrestrained (41).
uncouth: *adj* rude (62).
underlings: *n* subordinates (62).
unfettered: *adj* free (190).
unflinching: *adj* relentless (207).
unison: *n* harmony (12).
unkempt: *adj* untidy (7).
unmitigated: *adj* absolute (83, 205).
unperturbed: *adj* composed (206).
unwarranted: *adj* unnecessary (66).
unwieldy: *adj* awkward (134).
urbane: *adj* elegant (142).
usurped: *v* seized (37).
utility: *n* usefulness (87).

utilize: *v* use (175).
utopia: *n* perfection (223).

V

vacillating: *v* wavering (163).
vacuous: *adj* empty-headed (41).
valiant: *adj* brave (50).
valid: *adj* truthful, accurate (21).
valor: *n* courage (162).
vapidity: *n* lifelessness (9).
variegated: *adj* multicolored (49).
vehemently: *adv* forcefully (21).
veneer: *n* coating (69).
venerable: *adj* respected (99).
verbose: *adj* wordy (2).
verdant: *adj* green (38).
verdict: *n* judgment (49).
veritable: *adj* genuine (89).
verve: *n* vitality (127).
vexing: *adj* bothering (7).
vicariously: *adv* experience secondhand (5).
vicinity: *n* direction (125).
vilify: *v* slander (190).
vitriol: *n* rage (37).
vituperating: *v* berating (92).
vivacity: *n* liveliness (24).
vividly: *adv* clearly (128).
vocation: *n* career or profession (174).
vowed: *v* promised (50).
vulnerable: *adj* open to attack (145).

W

wallow: *v* roll around (35).
waned: *v* declined (215).
wary: *adj* cautious (38).
whim: *n* impulse (131).
wielding: *v* carrying (41).
winsome: *adj* charming (42).
wistfully: *adv* sadly (125).
wrath: *n* anger (12).
wreak: *v* inflict (150).
wrested: *v* tore (69).
wretched: *adj* miserable (22).

Y

yoked: *v* bound (65).

Z

zeal: *n* enthusiasm (49).
zephyr: *n* breeze (33).

SPARKNOTES
Test Prep

Our study guides provide students with the tools they need to get the score they want...Smarter, Better, *Faster*.

Guide to the SAT & PSAT
1-4114-0150-6

SAT Critical Reading & Writing Workbook
1-4114-0434-3

SAT Math Workbook
1-4114-0435-1

10 Practice Tests for the SAT
1-4114-0467-X

10 Practice Exams for the SAT Subject Tests
1-4114-9823-2

Guide to the ACT
1-4114-0245-6

ACT English & Reading Workbook
1-4114-9675-2

ACT Math & Science Workbook
1-4114-9676-0

AP Power Pack: Biology
1-4114-0286-3

AP Power Pack: Calculus
1-4114-0288-X

AP Power Pack: Chemistry
1-4114-0290-1

AP Power Pack: Psychology
1-4114-0487-4

AP Power Pack: English Language and Composition
1-4114-9682-5

AP Power Pack: English Literature and Composition
1-4114-0485-8

AP Power Pack: U.S. History
1-4114-0289-8

AP Power Pack: European History
1-4114-0488-2

AP Power Pack: World History
1-4114-0486-6

AP Power Pack: U.S. Government and Politics
1-4114-0292-8